A Pastor's Heart

Katharine Wool Parrish

DEDICATION

This love story is dedicated
to all pastors who cherish
their call to Gospel ministry

ACKNOWLEDGMENTS

Many thanks go to church historians, librarians, faithful keepers of family records, and county clerks, for invaluable information on the births, deaths and struggles of ancestors who witnessed God's good Providence throughout their lives; To Six Serious Scribes who listened to and critiqued this manuscript; To Colleen Parrish, without whose patient love, technical expertise, and long hours of dedicated work this story would have never been published.

To God be the Glory

TABLE OF CONTENTS

Chapter 1

WEDDING PARTY

For nearly a hundred years, the rise and fall of Virginia politics was celebrated at Great Oaks, the imposing ancestral home of Tazewell County's sheriff Ben Thomas.

On a warm spring day in the year 1900, however, a different kind of history was being made. Ben's niece, Kate Kelly, was about to be married, and the wives and daughters of every influential family in the Valley were gathered to shower the bride with gifts of china, silver, crystal and linens. Seated on the empire-style, pale rose couch were the bride's two aunts, Rachel and Ella. Both widowed, they lived together in a small house belonging to their brother. Each wore a dark velvet frock with heavy cream lace at the neck and edging the long sleeves, a stark contrast to the "afternoon dresses" of tissue taffeta and voile, in pastel colors, the floor-length skirts fluffed out by hoops and petticoats.

"Sarah dear," Aunt Ella addressed her youngest niece, "daffodil-yellow is your color, with your red hair and green eyes. I wonder, though, if you're not in danger of catching a spring cold, with that neckline." Her nose twitched a bit as Sarah squirmed in her chair.

"Ella, my daughter is wearing the very latest style out of Washington City. I talked with Mrs. Hamilton about her fitting myself." Rachel smiled condescendingly at her sister. "You, of course, wouldn't know about today's styles, since you have no children of your own."

"I believe it's time to open your gifts, dear," the bride's mother spoke up.

Kate sat in a high-backed velvet chair beside the huge fireplace, her abundant chestnut hair piled on her head in the fashion of the day. Her light blue voile dress, with its intricate lace yoke and high neck, featured a delicate blue bow at her throat. A small corsage of pink sweetheart roses from her aunt's garden nestled by her left shoulder. She tugged at the ribbon on a large package.

"Just go ahead and break it," cried Sarah.

"Why?" asked Esther, Kate's younger sister.

"Because, silly, every broken ribbon means a baby."

The group dissolved into giggles, and Kate's face turned crimson. Her mother sat beside her, hands folded in her lap, trying to ignore this improper talk from the younger generation.

"Oh, Aunt Rachel, thank you." The bride pushed tissue paper from around a stunning cut glass bowl. "It will be beautiful on my dining table, with flowers in it."

Her aunt beamed. "Only the best for my charming niece," she murmured among the "ooh's and aah's" of the guests.

"Now open mine, Kate." Aunt Ella, pushed forward a larger box. Dutifully, Kate took the gift, slipped off the ribbon and tore at the wrapping paper. "Oh, it's a cut glass pitcher, and four glasses. Thank you, Aunt Ella." She unwrapped each one, placing them on a nearby table.

Ella settled back with a sigh and glanced at her sister, who turned quickly away.

Kate suddenly remembered that she had been given the middle name of Rachella after both of these doting aunts, for a reason.

When the gifts were all opened, and the ribbons made into a bouquet for Kate's rehearsal, the guests were invited into the dining room where silver platters filled with dainty sandwiches and sweets were waiting, along with foaming punch, in a crystal bowl. As the ladies settled back in the parlor with plates on their laps, the conversation soon turned to questions about the groom.

Before Kate could answer, her sister Esther spoke, a slight edge to her young voice. "He's a preacher. Hasn't a penny to his name, I hear."

"Now, Dear," her mother said. "Remember, Kate's Jonathan comes from a very wealthy family in the Tidewater area." She looked around, making sure the information was absorbed by all the women present.

"Even so, I was terribly offended by the rude behavior of those five brothers, at Cousin Abigail's party, in Norfolk," Esther complained. "I don't care if one of them is a lawyer. I thought they were all loud and uncouth."

"Esther, dear," her mother soothed, trying to gain control of the conversation, "they are young men, probably not brought up in the same way as your brothers." She hid a small smile behind her handkerchief. "But it was a time of celebrating, and I believe they were happy for their brother."

Rachel huffed. "They should be, considering the family he's marrying into."

"But he gave up his family fortune, to be a preacher, a traveling preacher at that. What kind of life is that for our Kate?" Esther tossed her golden curls.

"Oh, my dear, you can help him with his sermons, since you are a teacher," Ella cooed.

"She'll probably have to play the piano for all his services, don't you think?" Esther added.

Kate laughed. "He isn't marrying me to put me to work. It's because he loves me. And I love him." A mist filled the deep brown eyes.

"Oh, Kate. That is so romantic. Tell us about this beau of yours. He seems so formal, at church." Sarah scooted her chair closer to her cousin's.

Kate smiled. "He's quite cultured, and very shy, as a matter of fact." She shot a look at her sister. "When we first began courting, we would sit before the fire in the parlor and he would read poetry—Byron, Shelley, Keats and Browning." She looked down. "After a few evenings, he began to read only the love poems."

"How long did it take him to propose?" Sarah was on the edge of her chair.

Kate looked away. "He began preaching in our church in September, and he always stayed here at Uncle Ben's, when it was preaching Sunday."

"And Kate was living with us during the winter, teaching our children. Sarah was at finishing school in Tazewell." Kate's Aunt Faith added, "And besides, when the fifth baby arrived, I had my hands full."

Laughter rippled across the group as Kate continued. "We talked some at church, about the music and all. I began to pray he'd ask Papa if he could court me, and he must have, because one Saturday night Uncle Ben laid a fire, here in the parlor and told me not to keep the preacher up too late."

"Oh, I love this story." Sarah said, shivering with excitement. "Why haven't we heard it before?"

"Because I only just became engaged, and you just got home from school." She squeezed her cousin's hand. "Anyway, that night he read some poetry and we talked a while, but I went to my room early. I loved him already, but I didn't want to seem too forward."

Faith nodded her head. "We all knew he was smitten with our Kate. He couldn't take his eyes off her at church."

"I remember the Sunday morning---it was just after Christmas--when he dropped his notes and could hardly get through the sermon," Aunt Rachel put in.

Kate laughed. "And I was having trouble concentrating on the hymns. You see, he proposed the night before, but I told him I'd give him an answer the next day."

"Oh Kate, how did you stand it?" Sarah asked.

4

"It was hard, but I didn't want him to think I was in a hurry to get married."

"Well, you are almost twenty-six," Esther reminded her.

Kate glanced at her sister. "That afternoon, he asked me to go riding in his buggy. He proposed again, and I told him yes." The room was quiet, until Kate said, "I saw tears in his eyes. He said he couldn't understand how someone like me could love an 'old preacher' like him." She dabbed at her eyes with a dainty lace handkerchief.

Rachel raised her chin. "He must be very different when he's with you, than when he's in the pulpit."

"Actually, he's the same. He loves God with a passion I never saw in anyone else, and he truly cares about the folks in his churches."

"But he travels around all the time. How will you keep up with all those people?" Esther scolded.

"Will you travel with him? The trains are so noisy, and dirty," Aunt Ella commented, wrinkling her nose slightly.

"I'll go with him wherever God calls him to go," Kate answered.

Her mother laid a hand on Kate's arm as she addressed the group again. "Did you know that Jonathan is considering a pastorate in a city in North Carolina?"

"They can't move from the Valley. What will Kate's piano students do?" Aunt Rachel's voice quivered a little.

"When will we ever see you, Kate?" Susan's eyes were filling with tears.

"I told you," said Kate. "I'll go with Jonathan Woolridge wherever God calls him to go."

Chapter 2

AT HOME IN THE MANSE

Kate stood at the dining room table arranging pink camellias in the cut glass bowl, her Aunt Rachel's wedding gift.

"You feeling better this afternoon, Miss Woolridge? The preacher looked real lonesome at this big table eating his dinner." Louisa, the tiny, energetic housekeeper at the manse, had a look of real concern on her smooth brown face. Her husband, Nathaniel, was the church's custodian, and the couple had been taking care of Oxford's First Presbyterian Church, and its pastors, for many years.

"Yes, I think so, thank you, Louisa." Kate touched the delicate blossoms. "Wasn't Mrs. Bullock kind to bring these lovely camellias from her yard? Nothing else is blooming, it seems."

Louisa slid her dust cloth over the table and sideboard, careful to lift and replace the cut glass pitcher and glasses, Aunt Ella's gifts, displayed on the embroidered runner made by Kate's mother. "Yes Ma'am," she said, and a look of mischief brightened her eyes. "You mind now, when Miss Hearn comes with a bouquet just like those. They's cousins that married cousins, and they don't never let one get ahead of the other."

She finished dusting and said, "Gone be Christmas soon,

and folks in this church sho'ly know how to decorate this old house. You wait and see. You won't have to lift a finger." She went off humming, and soon Kate heard pans clattering in the kitchen.

Kate sighed, trying to ignore a wave of nausea. She made her way to the living room and sat on the overstuffed settee. Looking around, she thought, *I love these high ceilings and tall windows, the wide-planked floors and the long curving staircase.* However, she knew in her heart that it wasn't the house that gave her this deep sense of happiness, but being the wife of Jonathan Woolridge. He was a busy man, preparing sermons, visiting the congregation, working in his beloved woodworking shop. But he always had time for Kate. A prayer of gratitude formed in her heart. *Father in heaven, thank You for my husband, and for our sweet morning times, when we can read Scripture and pray together for our families and people in the church.* Of course, lately, mornings for Kate had been spent in bed, or with her head over the slop jar.

She rose and went to the kitchen. "Louisa, you're a wonder." She watched the woman slide a large pan into the oven. "I don't know how I would have gotten this place ready for Mother's visit last week. You had everything spotless." She laughed. "Mama and Esther tried hard to find something to criticize about my housekeeping, but they couldn't find a thing. Thank you for keeping my secret." Her grin was conspiratorial.

Louisa used a short poker to lift the stove lid, punched up the fire and added a stick of wood from the box nearby. Brushing her hands on her apron, she turned toward Kate, a smile on her face. "It was my pleasure, and you weren't feelin' so 'pert', you know." She headed toward the pantry, adding "I hope they'll come again. Your mama's very pretty, like you." Then, afraid she had said too much, she turned and filled her apron with potatoes.

Kate walked toward the stairs. She heard footsteps overhead, indicating to her that Jonathan had completed work on his sermon and was preparing for the afternoon's visits. "Is

Nathaniel hitching up Nellie?" she called over her shoulder.

"Yes Ma'am, the preacher done asked him about that."

In their bedroom, he was standing by the window, staring outside. That's when she saw them, the feathery flakes of the winter's first snow.

"Jonathan?" she was careful as she broke into his reverie, remembering that her husband was a deep thinker, often working out parts of his sermons while staring out a window, or riding in his buggy.

He turned to her with a smile and held out his arms. She went into them and snuggled against his chest, reminded again of how much she loved this man God had given her.

"Look, my dear," he said, his voice almost reverent. "The first snow. There's something magical about it."

She followed his gaze. "The first one of our marriage." She said, and frowned a little.

"What is it, Kate?" he asked. "Are you still feeling ill?"

"I'm feeling better today, but it's so early for snow. Will it be a long winter, do you think?"

Jonathan shrugged and held her close. "Maybe, but spring will come, and then you can enjoy the flowers from all the bulbs you planted along the front walk."

"And the wisteria on the back fence. It was glorious when we arrived last summer."

He gazed into her eyes. "Do you know that we've been married for exactly half a year? It seems I've loved you forever, and I'll never get enough of holding you like this."

She leaned back in his arms. "Jonathan, there is something very special about this first snow." She laughed a little at the question in his eyes. "And I am looking forward to spring, because there will be a little one in our house come May."

He stared at her. "That's. . .that's why you've been sick?"

She nodded.

"Oh, my dear one. Are. . .are you sure? Do we need to call Dr. Halifax?" She shook her head and wiggled out of his arms. "I'm as sure as a woman can be. When Mother was here last week, she confirmed my suspicious."

He looked so worried that she said, "Oh Jonathan, I really wanted you to be the first to know about our baby, but I wasn't sure until Mother and I talked. I hope you understand."

He turned and began to pace, his hands folded under his chin. "It's wonderful news. I didn't dare dream, at my age . . ." She heard awe in his voice. "It's just so soon. We haven't been married a year yet, and I'm not sure I'm ready to share my heart with anyone else, even our own child."

Kate laughed and reached for his hand. "You won't have to share me for a few more months yet, and by then we'll both be ready to welcome this little one into our happy life here at the manse." She glanced at the swirling snowflakes.

"Mother wants me to go home to the Valley, to have the baby. She'd like me to go to Tazewell, to the hospital."

He turned. "What did you tell her? Are you going?"

"Oh no. I want to have this baby right here, in our home." She walked over to the cherry bed, with its high arched headboard, and touched the fruit carvings there. "Right here in our bed, the one your father carved, and where you were born." Her smile was radiant.

"But is it safe? I've known of women who suffered in childbirth. Some even died."

"Oh, Jonathan," she said giving him a kiss on his smooth cheek, and giggling when his mustache tickled her lips. "You worry entirely too much. You're thinking of the Royster baby. Abigail was frail and the baby came early. I'm perfectly healthy, and Dr. Halifax's nurse is an experienced midwife." She grinned at him. "Just think about the joy of a sweet baby to love and rock in that beautiful chair you're making for me. Who knows, it may be a boy who will follow you around and even ride with you as you make your pastoral calls. You can teach him woodworking in your shop."

"Yes, yes, I suppose," he said, the lines in his face relaxing a bit. "But now, you need your rest." He retrieved his gold watch from a vest pocket. "I promised to go by the Henderson's' this afternoon. Their twin sons want to join our church, and I must make sure they are grounded in the Word and know what this step means."

"Of course, Jonathan. You go ahead. Mrs. Johnson is coming over later. Amanda is here from Raleigh, and I'm so happy to have a visit with her." She patted his arm. "I promise to rest for a while before they come." She sat on the bed. "Perhaps they'll be here when you get back. I know you were concerned about Amanda and her plans to marry that attorney she met."

"Yes, yes," he said absently, and came and sat beside here, enfolding her in his arms again. "Oh my dear, dear one," he whispered into her hair. "What a gift you are to me."

Kate kissed him and said, "Now go and make your calls before it gets dark. Louisa put a chicken in the oven, so our supper will be ready when you get home."

He studied her face for a moment, then kissed her soundly, before heading for the stairs. At the front door he picked up his coat and hat from the hall tree and went out to his carriage, where Nathaniel was waiting with the horse,

She watched from the window as he left the lane and started toward Oxford's main street.

"Oh Father in heaven," she prayed aloud, "How can I be so blessed? To have a good man who loves me, and . . ." she placed a hand on her flat stomach, "a baby coming in the spring, to share that love. Please let me give him a son to grow up just like his father, with a pastor's heart."

Chapter 3

A NEW JOY

"Pastor, you were right to fetch me when you did. This baby will be born before the day is over," Helen, the midwife smiled at the frenzied husband. "Now, you just go down to the kitchen and tell Louisa to put on some water to boil and bring me some clean linens. She knows what to do, and you pour yourself a cup of her coffee and try to relax."

"But my wife . . . Kate . . ."

"Kate is fine. She's a healthy woman and her baby has a strong heartbeat. This is women's work, so you just wait downstairs. I'll send word as soon as the baby comes." As Jonathan turned, glancing over his shoulder at the bed where his wife lay smiling and then suddenly grimacing in pain, Helen added, "Won't hurt to pray, Pastor." She closed the door on his retreating steps.

Earlier that morning, when Kate first woke him, he was terrified by the pain on her face, but she simply said, "It's time. Go and get the midwife." The baby was expected a week earlier, and Helen had come by to check on Kate several times, but now, in the first hours of May 11, 1901, Kate's pains began in earnest.

Jonathan hovered over her, even as he pulled on his clothes. "Mama is here, right down the hall. You go on and get

Helen. I'm sure she's expecting you." Kate tried to smile, but a pain gripped her. "Go!" she said, relaxing before the next pain.

Thirty minutes later Jonathan returned with the midwife and was unceremoniously sent to the kitchen. He found Louisa building up the fire and starting a pot of coffee. A lamp was lit on the large, round table. As he entered, she came out of the pantry with a kettle which she took to the sink and began pumping water.

"Morning, Preacher," she said. "I knowed this was the day. The Lord woke me early, and I figured I better come on to the house." She glanced at him over her shoulder. "Now don't you worry. Miss Helen's the best there is, and she's delivered many a healthy baby in this town. Just set yourself down. Coffee's almost ready."

Pale morning light was beginning to filter through the kitchen windows. It would be a beautiful spring day.

"Helen said she needed you to heat water and . . ."

"And bring some clean linens," she finished for him as she set the heavy pot on the stove. Louisa laughed. "Miss Helen an' me, we been delivering babies for a lot of years, some of them in this very house." She set a cup and saucer before him and left the room.

The pastor folded his arms on the table and rested his head, "O Lord God," he cried out, "Please protect my wife and baby. Bring her through this valley of the shadow of death." Tears filled his eyes. He heard a muffled scream and jumped up, heading for the steps.

Louisa met him. "It's just the labor, Preacher. All women scream, but it'll be over soon. Let's us get on back to the kitchen. I need some help with that kettle."

Obediently, Jonathan followed her to the kitchen. Another scream ripped his heart.

"Careful Preacher," Louisa said, as she lifted the steaming kettle off the stove and handed it to him "Let's get these things upstairs." She filled her arms with clean towels.

Glad to be useful, Jonathan balanced the heavy kettle and climbed the stairs as another scream split the air. Kate's mother opened the door and took the big pot from him. He strained to look at Kate. "She's fine," she said. "The pains are coming fast now. We'll have a baby soon."

"Ma—ma!" a loud wail came from the big bed, and the door closed.

He felt completely desolate, helpless for the first time in his life, and terrified. *What if she bleeds to death? What if the baby dies? What if I lose Kate, who has become dearer than life to me?* He stumbled toward the stairs.

Louisa insisted he eat breakfast, and afterward he escaped to his study, a small room built onto the house with its own entrance.

He didn't know how long he sat before his open Bible, seeing nothing.

As the clock was striking twelve, a knock sounded on the door to the hall, and Jonathan raced to open it, hoping for news.

Louisa's kind eyes met his, and she held a tray covered with a linen napkin. "Preacher, I brought you some sandwiches and a cup of coffee." As she set the tray on his desk, she said, "You got company. A buggy just pulled up outside. I'll fetch some more food." She was leaving when he heard a knock on the outside door and went to answer it.

"Samuel. Come in. I didn't know you were in town."

Samuel White, an old friend and fellow pastor, gripped Jonathan's hand and said, "We've been over at Stem, visiting Mary's grandmother. Dr. Halifax dropped by and told us you had been to fetch his nurse very early this morning."

Samuel looked into his friend's eyes. "How are you handling this, brother?"

Jonathan shook his head. "Not well. I never thought it would be so hard on Kate. And it's taking so long." He glanced at the mantle clock.

Samuel crossed the room and seated himself on the ancient leather couch. Jonathan, seeing the tray, said, "Forgive me.

May I offer you a little lunch? Louisa insists that I eat, and some company would be good." At the same moment the door opened on Louise and another tray.

Samuel reached over and took a coffee cup from her tray and helped himself to a sandwich. "Thank you, Louisa. This is very kind of you."

The woman, who had known Samuel's family for years, nodded and asked, "How is Miss Mary feeling today?"

"Holding her own, the doctor says, though she's suffered a serious bout with pneumonia."

"I'm sorry to hear she's ailing," Louisa said, and looked in Jonathan's direction. "Make sure my preacher eats something, Mr. Samuel." She turned and was gone.

"The women seem to be in charge today," said Jonathan, sipping his coffee. "They keep sending me away and saying, 'This is women's work'."

Samuel sat back. "I remember those times," he said. "Makes us husbands feel absolutely useless."

"Yes," Jonathan replied, relieved to have an understanding friend. Sandwich in hand, he began pacing.

"The first baby always seems to take longer. I remember our first one. Mary was in labor for twelve hours."

Jonathan stared at his friend. "That long? How did she stand it?"

Samuel smiled. "I don't know, but when that baby comes, it doesn't seem to matter." He shook his head. "It's one of God's mysteries, and we men can't begin to fathom it."

A quiet knock sounded, and Helen stepped into the room. Instantly Jonathan was at her side. She laid a hand on his arm. "No baby yet, Pastor." She smiled reassuringly. "I wanted you to know that Nathaniel has gone for the doctor."

"Something's wrong. What . . .?" Jonathan stammered.

"Not really, Pastor. The baby is breech, which means that it is not in a good position for the head to slide into the birth canal."

The pastor sank into his chair, his face ashen. The nurse

14

continued. "Kate is tired, and we're doing all we can to get the baby to turn. These births take longer, and I just wanted Dr. Halifax to be here with us." She touched his arm. "She's going to be fine, Pastor, but a little more prayer won't hurt." She nodded at Samuel and was gone.

Samuel stood and laid a hand on his friend's shoulder. "Let me pray for you, my brother," he said.

They knelt by the old sofa, as Jonathan's friend from seminary days prayed for God's mercy, His guidance for the doctor and nurse, and health for Kate and her baby.

Rising, he embraced Jonathan and said, "I must be going. Mary is anxious to return to Raleigh for our daughter's program at her school this evening." He looked into Jonathan's worried eyes. "You are in no shape to preach this Sunday. I'll send my assistant, James Spruill, up. He's young, but has the makings of a good pulpit man. I'm sure your people will love him. And you will let us know about the baby?"

"Yes, certainly. And thank you, Samuel," he said, opening the door. As his friend climbed into the waiting buggy, Jonathan silently thanked God for the gift of friendship.

He didn't know how long he sat at his desk. Perhaps he slept, for when he raised his head off his arms, the room was dark and he noticed someone had lighted a lamp on the table by the couch. As the clock began to strike, he heard a faint cry. Then another, stronger one. He jumped up. *The baby! His child!*

He bounded up the steps and was greeted by a smiling Louisa. "Go see your baby, Preacher," she said, and slipped past Jonathan, headed for the kitchen.

Suddenly he was paralyzed. The room was quiet, except for the child's mewling cry. Yet there was excitement and awe, a feeling of relief, and concern at the same time. Helen and Dr. Halifax, over at the window, conferred in quiet tones.

He went straight to the bed where Kate lay, weak but smiling. He bent to kiss her cheek and stroked her hair as tears coursed down his cheeks. Beside his wife lay a small bundle. "Would you like to see your son?" she asked.

15

His son! Kate had given him a boy! He pulled the corner of the blanket away from the tiny, red face and gazed at it. Blinking away tears, he choked out, "He looks like his mother."

Dr. Halifax came and laid a hand on his shoulder. "Congratulations, Jonathan. You have a perfect son." He shook his head. "We almost lost both of them, but God has been good to us this long day."

Jonathan continued to stare at the miracle before him.

"What will you name him?" asked the doctor.

"He is James Craig Woolridge the second, after my father." Jonathan's voice trembled a little.

The bundle began to wail, and Kate's mother came to take him. "We need to give this young man his first bath."

Jonathan leaned over the bed and placed a kiss on Kate's cool forehead. He tucked away damp curls from her temple. "Thanks be to God," he whispered. the tears coming again.

The doctor was putting instruments into his bag. "I'm going back to my office. Kate, you need to get some rest. Helen will stay with you." He shook the pastor's hand and left.

Jonathan floated down the stairs. He had a son. And God had spared Kate's life. He returned to his study where he prostrated himself before his God in tearful, grateful prayer.

Later, in the hallway, he sniffed the tantalizing aroma of vegetable soup and warm bread. He was suddenly ravenous.

Early the next morning, Jonathan was at the telegraph office. "We heard you had a fine boy, Preacher," said the operator. "Bet you're here to send some telegrams with the good news."

"That's right, Anderson. I need to let my family know how God has blessed us."

He wrote out the message he would send to his mother and brothers, to Kate's father, and to his friend Samuel. It read: "James Craig Woolridge II born to Jonathan and Kate May 11, 1901. May God be praised."

Chapter 4

A SUDDEN SORROW

The house was too quiet. Jonathan, trying hard to concentrate on his sermon preparation, found his mind wandering to the bedroom upstairs where Kate lay resting. She had been up several times in the last few days, sitting in the new rocker to nurse baby James Craig. She even came downstairs one day, and ate with him. Each time, however, she seemed to be exhausted by the least activity, and took to her bed again. It was almost two weeks since the birth. Shouldn't Kate be regaining her strength? She was so frail. He had questioned the midwife, who came regularly to check on both her charges, and she always assured him that, after a difficult birth like Kate's, it would take time to recover.

He had hardly been able to see his son. Grandmother Kelly took over the baby's care, and was bathing and dressing him—even taking him out for short strolls in the wicker carriage the church had given them.

He started at the knock on his study door. "Preacher," Louisa said, "Dr. Halifax is here. I'll bring ya'll some coffee."

Jonathan didn't like the look on the doctor's face as he entered the study. They both sat on the old couch.

"Thank you for coming, Doctor," he said. "I believe you've been here every day this week. I'm sure you have other patients who need you."

The doctor nodded as Louisa placed a tray with two steaming mugs on the table and left.

As the door closed, Dr. Halifax cleared his throat and spoke, "Pastor, I'm afraid the news is not good."

Jonathan's hands began to shake, and his palms grew sweaty. He looked into the doctor's eyes. "What do you mean?"

The doctor sighed and took a sip of his coffee. "Kate is not responding as she should be. In fact, she's getting weaker by the day."

"But Helen said it would take some time for her to regain her strength after the difficult labor."

Doctor Halifax shook his head. "Yes, but it's nearly two weeks now, and Kate continues to hemorrhage. I've tried everything I know, and she simply grows weaker." He sighed. "She's lost too much blood."

"Should we get her to a hospital, maybe even take her to Raleigh?"

The doctor's eyes were full of compassion. "She's too weak to be moved, Jonathan." his tone was sorrowful.

Anger and helplessness raged in Jonathan. He stood and began pacing the floor, slamming his fists into his palms. "There must be something we can do."

"I've sent for Helen to come and stay around the clock." He put a gentle hand on the pastor's arm. "But, Pastor, I'm afraid you must prepare yourself . . ."

"No!" Jonathan roared.

The door opened, and Helen's tear-splashed face told him what he didn't want to know.

He tore past her, up the stairs, to the silent room where his wife lay in the big cherry bed.

She was so still under the coverlet.

Jonathan threw himself on her, begging her to respond. He began to weep—wild, convulsive sobs torn from the depths of his soul.

He was aware that others were moving quietly about them.

From another room he heard his son's cries of hunger, but was powerless to move.

Some time later, Louisa came in to light a lamp on the bedside table. Dr. Halifax grasped Jonathan's shoulder and helped him to the rocker. Then he bent over the bed, listened for a moment with his stethoscope, and gently placed the sheet over Kate's quiet face.

He turned to the pastor. "She's gone."

He pulled up a chair and sat beside the bereaved husband.

Lost in unbelief and grief, Jonathan sat motionless.

Finally, the doctor stood. "I've called the elders, and Helen will stay until someone from the church comes," he said, and left.

Jonathan became aware of a baby's shrill screams, and then all was quiet. He didn't know that Louisa, knowing what was about to happen, went early in the day to visit her cousin who had given birth the week before.

In a small frame house on the edge of town, a young black girl opened the door to Louisa and the grief-stricken grandmother.

"Mama's in the bedroom," the child said and led them to a back room where Della, seated in a pine rocker, opened her arms.

"Miss Kelly, this is my cousin Della," Louisa said, taking the small wailing bundle from his grandmother's arms and placing the child in Della's lap.

Della wept as she guided the small hungry mouth to her abundant breast. "Poor motherless child," she cooed. "Della got plenty of milk for two babies. You take all you need."

The young girl had brought two cane chairs into the room, and the visitors sat.

"Awful good of you to take this baby to feed, Della. Don't know what we'd do without you."

"Louisa, you know I always have plenty of milk for my babies." She smiled and glanced at a large basket by the bed. "You shoulda' heard my Lester burp a while ago. He was full as a tick."

Louisa turned to Mrs. Kelly. "Della's birthed six babies, and wet-nursed I don't know how many more. The Lord's been good to us this day, 'cause that little one is hungry." She spoke to Della, who had removed the baby from her breast and put him on her shoulder. Soon they heard a satisfied burp, and Della gave him her other breast. "He's getting what he needs, finally. His mama, God rest her sweet soul. . ." Louisa had to stop and swipe at a rush of tears. "She tried to nurse him, but she was so weak, her milk didn't satisfy him."

Della laughed softly as she cuddled the suckling child. "He's making up for it now. This baby's gonna be a healthy boy before you know it."

Half an hour later, Louisa helped the grandmother into the waiting buggy and handed her a sleeping infant. Climbing in beside them, she said to Nathaniel. "Can you fetch Della to the manse when we need her again?" Nathaniel nodded, and so began a daily round of visits as the child flourished on Della's milk.

Later, Louisa took sandwiches and coffee to the study where Jonathan had retreated. Two elders were with him and a man she recognized from the local funeral parlor. She set the tray down and said, "Preacher, excuse me, but I thought you'd want to know, me and Miss Kelly took your baby to my cousin's house so she could feed him. He's sleeping good in his cradle upstairs. She's coming again, every day, long as we need her. We gonna' take good care of that precious baby boy." Her voice quivered, and she turned to leave.

Johnathan blinked, as though coming out of sleep. "Uh, thank you, Louisa. I . . . uh . . . I didn't even think . . ."

"I know, Preacher. Don't you worry about that." She slipped out of the room, as the men sat down and began to talk.

After a sleepless night, Jonathan walked to the court house

20

and purchased a plot in Oxford's Elmwood Cemetery. Like Abraham of old, who purchased a burial cave for his beloved wife Sarah, that piece of land was the only property Jonathan Woolridge ever owned.

Jonathan never knew how his friend got the word, but Samuel showed up the day after Kate died. He went over funeral plans with Jonathan, and returned the next day to officiate at the burial.

For weeks, Jonathan wandered in a state of unbelief. A few days after the funeral, he took Kate's mother to board the train home to Virginia. He struggled to concentrate on sermon preparation, and to interact with the members of his flock who came by with food and offers of help.

One morning, a month after the funeral, he wandered into the dining room and overheard a conversation.

"Louisa, you need some rest. You're here before day, and working late in the night. When you gonna' slow down, gal?"

Louisa sighed, "These be hard times, Nathaniel. We'll get some rest when the baby's older. Right now, the Preacher needs us, so we claim the grace of God and go on."

Jonathan was stricken. *What have I done to these two loyal servants?*

He opened the kitchen door and was greeted with a big smile. "Morning, Preacher" said Louisa. "Ready for a nice big breakfast?"

"Why, yes. Thank you." He sat down and reached for the cup of coffee she offered him. A kind of amazement registered on his face as he looked from Louisa to her husband. "How can I ever thank you, both of you? You've cared for my son for weeks now." He heard a soft gurgling sound from a basket near the stove, and leaned over to look.

"Go on, pick up your boy, Preacher. He's been needing his daddy." Louisa was flipping pancakes on a skillet.

Awkwardly, Jonathan bent over and lifted the bundle. He held his son close, as tears coursed down his cheeks. At the stove, Louisa was choking back a sob.

Later that day, the pastor wrote to his mother. His father had died several years earlier, and she was living alone in Norfolk. Perhaps she would come for a few weeks to help with the child's care.

Chapter 5

ROCK-A-BYE

Louisa entered the study where Jonathan sat at his desk, now strewn with open books and pages of scribbled sermon notes.

"Preacher, here's a nice tall glass of iced tea to cool you off, and a slice of Miss Webb's pound cake to go with it."

"Thank you, Louisa," the pastor said absently, never looking up at her or the tray she set on the table by the couch.

The fact was, his only solace, during these hot June days, was the Scripture, and his struggle to interpret it for his congregation.

As she left, Jonathan heard the front door bell.

Louisa opened the door and smiled at Lucy Webb.

"Good morning, Louisa," she said, entering the cool front hall. "I brought this for the baby."

With a question on her face, Louisa took the package.

"It's the baptismal dress that both my girls, and my granddaughters, wore," Lucy continued. "It's been on a shelf in my closet for years. Do you know if the pastor has made any plans for the baby's baptism?"

"No Ma'am. He ain't said nothing to me," Louisa answered, as she motioned toward the parlor and followed Lucy into the room.

"Well," sighed the visitor, seating herself on the settee. "I was thinking of them both, praying about what I could do to soften the grief, and the Lord reminded me of this dress. My mother made it, even tatted the lace, when my first baby was born. I would love to give it to the pastor for little James' baptism."

Louisa sat on a straight chair and blinked away tears as she opened the box and looked at the long, freshly-laundered dress of white lawn with wide lace inserts. Her voice was full of wonder as she said, "It's beautiful, Miss Webb. You sure you want to give away this family heirloom?"

"I'm sure, Louisa. The pastor is very dear to our family, and I want so much to help him get through this sad, difficult time."

"But you done sent I don't know how many meals, and cakes, and . . ."

Lucy laid a hand on Louisa's arm. "I pray this is a way God can love both the pastor and that dear baby, through us."

She rose to go, and Louisa, still holding the box, said, "Thank you, Miss Webb. I'll tell the preacher what you said."

The door closed and Louisa walked toward the study. She wondered how the pastor would respond to this act of extreme generosity and love toward him and his son.

Later, back in the kitchen, Louisa threw more wood into the stove in preparation for cooking the noonday meal. With the hem of her apron, she swiped perspiration from her face as she began peeling potatoes, her heart forming the words of a prayer. *Lord, that man's just pining away in that little old study room. He sits there every day, that old black coat and high collar on, reading and writing and thinking. How can he stand it, this hot weather, without a breath of air stirring in the house? Even when I showed him that beautiful baptismal dress, he just grunted, like he didn't even see it.*

She never noticed the big tear running down her face. "Oh Lord," she prayed aloud as the potato peelings fell into a bucket. "Please come and ease the pain in his sore heart. And that little baby, already a month old, and the preacher hardly ever held him since his mama died."

"You talking to the Lord about that baby again?" Nathaniel asked, as he came in the back door bringing wood for the stove.

"Nathaniel, those two need each other. How we gonna' get 'em together?" She put the pot of potatoes on the stove to cook and set about mixing up a meatloaf.

Nathaniel poured himself a glass of iced tea, took a bandanna out of his back pocket and wiped his face and neck, as he sat down at the table. "Now, Louisa, you're doing all you can, making sure that little one gets fed and changed, and whatever else he needs. I don't know how much longer you can do all that and the cooking and house tending too."

He rose and went to where she stood at the table, her hands in a deep bowl. He put his arms around her, and she relaxed against him. "Honey pie," he whispered, "I miss you."

"I know, Nathaniel, but what are we gonna' do? We can't let that sweet baby grow up without no loving at all."

"Well, Della's feeding him, and she loves him like she do her own." He sighed. "But it ain't right somehow."

He returned to the table and emptied his glass.

"You're right, Nathaniel. Guess we just need to pray harder, see what God's gonna' do."

In the quiet dining room, Louisa served the pastor's meal. He sat stiffly, as usual, dressed in his frock coat and high celluloid collar.

"Going out visiting today, Preacher?" she asked as she placed the fluffy potatoes on the table. "I heard a wagon this morning, and Mrs. Hearn's cook's boy come through my kitchen looking for you, just now."

"Yes, Louisa, I'll be making several calls this afternoon. Mr. Hearn is back down with a relapse of his pneumonia, and Mrs. Currin sent a message that she needed me to come and visit her mother." He took a bite of meatloaf before he spoke again.

"The Johnsons want to discuss their daughter's wedding in August."

"I'll leave your supper in the warming oven, then, and . . ."

A lusty cry sounded from upstairs, and Louisa turned toward the steps, asking, "Want I should bring the baby down, after I change him?"

Jonathan sighed. "Maybe that would be good. I've hardly seen him when he was awake." His smile was thin.

"And Louisa," he added, "I received a telegram this morning." She stopped and turned to face him. "My mother is coming in on the afternoon train, the day after tomorrow."

"How long she staying, Preacher?"

"She didn't say, but she's closed up the house, so I imagine she will be here for a few weeks."

Louisa's mind raced. That lady had never been to the manse. Would she approve of Louisa's housekeeping? As she flew up the stairs in answer to little James' cries, she began to plan a whirlwind housecleaning.

Later, as Louisa sat and rocked the baby after giving him a bottle of Della's milk, her husband entered the kitchen looking for another cool drink.

"Whew!" he said, "cleaning up that church house is a young man's job. I'm about wore out, and I still got the pews to polish tomorrow."

"You got something else to do tomorrow, too," Louisa said as she patted the child on her shoulder. "You and me gonna' clean this house from top to bottom."

Nathaniel stared at her. "What's got into you, woman? We just did the spring cleaning back in April. How dirty can it get, with just one man and one little baby living here?"

Louisa rocked for a few minutes, until she heard the child's soft, regular breathing.

"There's a woman coming."

"Lots of women come here, bringing food and such."

"I mean, there's a woman coming to *stay* here."

"Who?" Curious now, Nathaniel sat up straight in his chair.

"The preacher's mama. She's coming to take care of this baby, I expect." Louisa's voice trembled a little, and she dropped a kiss on the small head cradled in her hand.

"Did Mr. Woolridge complain about what we're doing for the boy?"

"No, Nathaniel. Sometimes I wonder if he even knows what we do, he's so full of sorrow."

"Then, why's she coming?"

"I don't know, but remember, we prayed for some help? Maybe the Lord's sending little James' grandma in answer to that prayer."

"Maybe so," he reflected, smiling. "It'll be a load off your shoulders, Louisa." Then he frowned. "But why we gotta' clean up the house?"

"I told you," Louisa said, as she placed James in his basket. "There's a woman coming."

Chapter 6

HELP ON THE WAY

Jonathan paced the platform, glancing now and then at the tracks where the train from Norfolk would be arriving. The anxiety mirrored in his face had not so much to do with the train's schedule as with his own heart. He had not seen his mother since his wedding, a year ago. He remembered her thinly-veiled disdain for Kate and her family. She had told his brothers that Jonathan was marrying into a family of "country people."

Now she was coming to visit—perhaps for several weeks— to help care for his motherless child. Would she be comfortable at the manse, accustomed as she was to a life of wealth and society? He remembered she had been a kind enough mother to all her six sons, but from the beginning, nurses and tutors were often closer to the boys, sharing their lives.

Elmira Demarest Woolridge was well-known as a leader in Norfolk society, but Jonathan had precious few memories of time spent with his mother. He winced as he remembered the reactions of both parents when he told them of his decision to answer a call to the Gospel ministry, rather than joining the family's furniture business, or becoming an attorney as his brother had done. His parents never visited him, not even for the dedications of five church buildings which housed congregations he had started, in southwestern Virginia. In the years since his father's death, however, John had sensed a new sadness in his mother's infrequent letters. It was difficult to picture his mother in that light, but his pastor's heart reached out to her, in spite of his trepidation about bringing her into his home.

As he paced, another thought hit him. Baby James was, after all, his mother's own flesh and blood, but how would she get along with Louisa and Nathaniel? He had seen the two servants scurrying around the old house these last two days, scrubbing, sweeping, beating rugs and draperies on the backyard clothesline, shining windows and mirrors, and spreading clean linens on all the beds. He thought the house was perfectly presentable, but Louisa was like a woman driven by the devil himself. Jonathan had all he could do to keep from reprimanding her, and he still wasn't sure where his notes for Sunday's sermon had landed.

As a faraway whistle heralded the train's approach, Jonathan breathed a prayer. *Lord, help me to show Your love to my mother. And please, stay between her and Louisa.*

The train came to a stop, with screeching brakes and a loud belch of steam. Jonathan searched the car windows and then heard his mother's voice. "Young man, be careful of that hat box. It contains the latest bonnet from Paris. And the trunk can be set on the platform. My son's man will load it onto his conveyance."

The pastor rushed to greet his mother, help her down the train's steps, and tip the long-suffering porter.

"Welcome to Oxford, Mother," he said, taking her arm and guiding her to the wagon where Nathaniel was climbing down, preparing to load the trunk.

Nathaniel groaned as he tugged at it, then called to a young man walking by.

"Jasper, come and help me with this here trunk." When they had lifted the trunk into the wagon, Nathaniel said to his helper,

"Climb on in. If you help me unload it and get it in the house, I'll ask Louisa to cut you a piece of that coconut cake she been working on."

Jasper laughed as he climbed into the wagon bed and both men made themselves comfortable beside the huge trunk. "I can't wait for a bite of Louisa's cake, she makes the best," Jasper grinned.

"Don't know what I'd do if you hadn't come along to help me with this big old trunk." Nathaniel kept his voice low.

"Good thing I was at the depot. Aunt Della sent me to see if her mail order package come." He shook his head. "No telling what she's gone and ordered this time."

Nathaniel shot a look at the wagon's wooden seat. "Reckon that lady ever rode in a wagon before?" he whispered.

"Don't know, but she's taking up most of the seat. The Preacher's about to fall off." Jasper stifled a chuckle.

Jonathan took up the reins and clucked to his horse.

"Did you have a pleasant trip, Mother?" he asked as they drove around the town square, toward the manse.

"Oh, it was terrible!" she answered, adjusting her hat. "Trains are loud and filthy. I wish there were another mode of transportation."

"I'm sorry, Mother," he tried to sound sincere, "but I'm glad you're here safe and sound. Your room is ready, so you can have a little rest before supper. I'm sure Louisa will have a good meal for us."

"I didn't come to rest, or to gorge myself on some servant's cooking, Son. I came to be of assistance to you and that child, in your time of need."

Jonathan sighed. "I know, Mother, and I do appreciate your sacrifice for us. Your grandson and I need you." He smiled but her dour expression never changed.

At the manse, the men jumped down and began unloading the trunk. Jonathan helped his mother down and grabbed the large hatbox from the wagon. He rushed to open the door for the men, who were already sweating, and they had not begun the long pull up the stairs.

The pastor thanked them as they passed him, and then welcomed his mother into his home.

She looked around. "Son, couldn't you even afford a decent settee for your parlor? That one looks as if it's been used."

Jonathan laughed. "It has, Mother. It was here when we moved in, along with most of the manse furnishings."

"Well, at least you have this hall table your brother made." She ran her gloved hand over the table's shining surface.

Jonathan overheard Nathaniel, coming down the stairs, speaking quietly to Jasper, "Sure am glad Louisa made a fuss about everything being clean." He grinned and added, "Come on, you just earned yourself a piece of cake and a tall glass of iced tea."

Elmira, pacing around the parlor, finally sat in the red brocade arm chair. "I'm so glad to see this chair being put to good use. I remember when your father had this suite of furniture made for our drawing room in New York." She sighed. "Those were the days. Guests for dinner every night, and musicales in the parlor afterward." She looked around. "I do so wish we could have kept this beautiful suite together, but none of you boys has a large enough house for a drawing room, so your father thought it best to divide it among the six of you."

"Would you care to go up and see your room now, so you can begin to unpack and get comfortable?"

Just then they heard a child's cry from upstairs and he continued, "I know you're anxious to meet the baby, but the wet nurse is with him now, I believe."

Laboriously, she rose from the chair and followed her son up the stairs.

"Did you say the child has a wet nurse? Of course, the poor little thing would need someone to feed and care for him. How did you obtain her?"

"Louisa, my housekeeper, brought her cousin Della in to help. It seems she had a child born about the same time as James."

Elmira's hand flew to the lace collar at her throat. "Do you mean to tell me that my grandson is being nursed by a *negro* woman?"

Jonathan stiffened as he answered, "Yes, Mother, and he seems to be thriving on Della's milk. I am very grateful."

"Well, I suppose . . . I mean, there's probably very little difference, but I wonder if it will affect his sensibilities when he's older."

"I can't imagine what you mean, Mother." He opened the door to a large bedroom where the men had placed the trunk. Jonathan looked at his mother and spoke, a slight edge to his voice, "As I said, I'm indeed grateful for these women who have cared for my son, and I very much hope you will appreciate them as well."

Chapter 7

COVENANT CHILD

"Jonathan, I'm speaking to you."

His mother's sharp voice brought the pastor out of a deep reverie.

"Yes, Mother?" he said, trying to concentrate on her face across the dinner table. Seeing her displeasure, he continued. "I . . . I'm sorry, Mother, I'm afraid my mind was on the plans for the Johnson's wedding on Saturday." He was struggling with this, his first wedding since Kate's death.

Having secured his attention, Elmira went on. "I've been thinking about the baby's christening."

Jonathan blinked. "His . . . Mother, in the Presbyterian Church, we call it 'infant baptism'."

"Well, whatever you want to call it, the child is almost four months old. It simply must be done soon. How does it look for the minister's own child to go this long without the blessing of the church? It's simply scandalous. I'm surprised you haven't attended to this already." She reached for a roll, as Louisa offered the warm basket.

The pastor recoiled at her criticism. "I . . . I suppose I'd never thought about it."

"Well. It's high time! You need to make plans for the service, before the child gets any older." Suddenly, she gave a small cry, and rested a hand over her heart. "What about a baptismal gown? We must have a proper gown for the ceremony. I may have to order one sent from home."

Louisa turned at the kitchen door. "We got a baptismal gown for baby James to wear," she said.

"We do?" Jonathan asked.

"Preacher, don' t you remember? I showed you the dress Miss Webb brought you."

"Oh, yes." Jonathan searched his thoughts. "The box . . . That was a baptismal gown?"

Both ladies heaved a sigh at the same time. "Oh, Jonathan, what would you do without me?" said his mother.

Then she turned to Louisa. "Where is this box with the gown?"

"In my study," answered Jonathan. "Would you like to see it?"

"Of course," she answered, taking a sip of water. "As soon as we've finished dinner."

Elmira's gnarled fingers glided over the soft folds of the dimity gown and fingered the heavy lace of the yoke.

Jonathan watched in amazement as his stern mother's countenance softened, and a tear slid down her cheek. "This is exquisite," she breathed. "And it was a gift? From a parishioner?"

Jonathan's own eyes clouded with tears, and he touched the long gown spread across his mother's lap. "Yes," he said, "I believe Mrs. Webb brought it by. She told Louisa it had been made for her daughters, and she wanted James to have it for his baptism."

Elmira turned to her son. "So why haven't you mentioned it? Were you not planning to have the child *baptized*?" The sternness was back.

"Well, yes, I suppose so. You see, I've been so busy . . ."

Elmira touched his arm, her voice gentle, "No, Son, you've been grieving. You lost your beloved wife." Another tear threatened, and she straightened up. "But now, I'm here and we'll attend to this right away."

"I'd like to ask Samuel White to preside," Jonathan said. "I'm not sure I could . . ."

"I understand," she answered, carefully folding the gossamer gown in its box. "Now, we need to plan a celebration. Maybe a light meal here at the manse, unless the ladies of the church want to do something, which, of course, they certainly should." She closed the box, laid it on the couch and rose.

Jonathan went to the telephone. "I'll call Samuel now, and we'll set a time for the service."

"And I'll take care of the women" she said, sweeping out of the room.

Late September sunshine slanted across the congregation. Jonathan stood with his friend before the pulpit and watched his mother come down the aisle carrying his son, swathed in the long, flowing gown. The baby squirmed, but seemed to know his grandmother expected him to keep quiet for this very important ceremony.

Jonathan struggled to control his emotions. His son, this child so like his beloved Kate, was coming to receive the promises of the Covenant.

He stepped to his mother's side. Samuel began with the question, "Do you acknowledge your child's need of the cleansing blood of Jesus Christ, and the renewing grace of the Holy Spirit?"

Jonathan gazed at his son and answered hoarsely, "I do."

"Do you claim God's covenant promises in his behalf, and do you look in faith, to the Lord Jesus Christ for his salvation, as you do for your own?"

"I do."

"Do you now unreservedly dedicate your child to God and promise, in humble reliance upon divine grace, that you will endeavor to set before him a godly example, that you will pray with and for him, that you will teach him the doctrines of our holy religion, and that you will strive, by all the means of God's appointment, to bring him up in the nurture and admonition of the Lord?"

Jonathan's voice was a little stronger, and rose above his child's whimper. "I do."

After a prayer, Samuel reached into a silver bowl held by a deacon, and sprinkled James' small head saying, "James Craig Woolridge II, I baptize thee in the name of the Father, and of the Son, and of the Holy Ghost." [1]

A few minutes later, Samuel stepped behind the pulpit to preach the morning's sermon, and in the church's balcony, Louisa held tightly to Nathaniel's arm, wiping away tears with her free hand.

1.*Presbyterian Book of Church Order, pp. 185–186 John Knox Press 1950*

Chapter 8

ALL IN A PASTOR'S DAY

A breeze from the open window rustled papers on his desk as the pastor consulted a passage in his Greek New Testament.

Jonathan relished the quiet of his study. The rest of the manse seemed to be always filled with commotion. If it was not a baby crying, it was people coming by to bring produce from their gardens, or Jonathan's mother complaining about her headaches.

James was barely a year old and already toddling around the house. Jonathan heard the sound of laughter as Louisa took James upstairs for an afternoon nap. He felt deep pride in his son, but still had difficulty relating to the child. The resemblance to his mother was heart-stabbing. He had her eyes, her smile, even the ear which, in spite of the cap his grandmother insisted upon, still stood away from the small head.

A few minutes later, a knock sounded on the door and Louisa slipped into the study. "Preacher," she said, "It's Miss Mary Webb. The Cap'n says she's took a turn for the worst. Their boy's in the kitchen, says they need you to come."

Jonathan looked up, his finger holding a place in the Scripture. "Have they called the doctor?"

"Don't know, Preacher, but they 'specially asked for you.

Anthony says she's bad off this time."

The pastor heaved a sigh, closed his book and stood. "Tell Anthony I'll be along shortly."

"Yes, Preacher," she said, as she left.

There had been many calls from his aging parishioner in the past six months, but this could be the end. Mrs. Webb, in her mid-nineties, lived with her son and his family on their plantation at Stem, just north of Oxford. Jonathan's friend Samuel had married one of her granddaughters. The other, Grace, was away teaching school somewhere in Virginia. Jonathan had heard a rumor that she was engaged to be married.

In the kitchen, Louisa poured a glass of milk for the young boy who sat stuffing himself with her pound cake. "Anthony, why ain't you in school today?" she asked.

"Cap'n Webb, he told me to stay home today so I could help with his crops." The young chest puffed out. "Now I'm twelve years old, they need me in the field." He said, with an air of authority. "Been raining so much, we need to reset the 'baccer and plant more maters." He stopped to finish off a second slice of cake and continued, "Then, he come to the field and holler, 'Anthony, run fast as you can to the barn. Jacob's taking the wagon to town. You go with him and fetch the preacher. Tell him Mrs. Webb failing fast this time'."

Louisa looked out the window. "Jacob setting out there in the hot sun all this time. Here, you take him some of this cake and fetch him a dipper of water from the porch." She wrapped the cake in a linen napkin and handed it to the boy. "Ya'll get on home, tell the Cap'n an' Miss Lucy the preacher's on his way." Closing the screen door behind the boy, Louisa noticed Jonathan heading toward the barn to hitch Nellie to his buggy.

As she turned back to the kitchen, she heard, "Louisa," and looked up to see the pastor's mother looming in the doorway.

"Didn't I tell you that I would require Jonathan to take me to Mrs. Doughtery's house for the committee meeting about the ladies' luncheon?"

"Yes, Ma'am, but the preacher just got a call to go to Mrs. Webb's sickbed. They say she's bad off this time."

"I declare, I can never plan anything, with Jonathan flitting off to visit sick parishioners at the drop of a hat." Elmira's tight hair bun seemed in danger of loosening under her black bonnet, as she shook her head in despair. "I must get to that meeting. Those ladies have no idea about the proper planning of these things."

"Don't you worry, Miss Woolridge. Nathaniel be here in a minute, for a glass of lemonade, and he'll be happy to take you out to Miss Doughtery's place, if you don't mind riding in the wagon."

"Very well, then. Please call me when he comes in." The older woman turned on her heel and left. Louisa struggled to suppress a giggle.

A moment later, the cries of a hungry child rang through the house. Louisa hurried up the stairs to the nursery where she greeted James, who was standing in his crib with a red face and a sagging diaper.

From the parlor, she heard Ellmira call. "Please do something about that child. His constant crying is giving me a headache."

Going to the crib, Louisa mumbled, "That woman's no help at all. She just wants folks to wait on her."

Then she smiled, as the child caught sight of her and stopped wailing. "You just need your Auntie Louisa, don't you, child?" She laid him in the crib and reached for a clean diaper on a nearby shelf. "We get you changed in a hurry, and then we go to Louisa's kitchen and get us some applesauce and oatmeal." She tickled the fat tummy as she changed him, and he laughed as she hoisted him onto her hip for the trip downstairs. "You such a big boy, won't be long before you come downstairs by yourself." She smiled at him, but her heart constricted, as she thought how soon these baby days would be over.

———— ♡ ————

The afternoon sun slanted through the cedar trees, as Jonathan steered his horse up the lane toward the Webb home place. The spacious colonial house named "Mount Welcome", had escaped the ravages of the War Between the States, and remained a center for social life in the small community of Stem. On the wide veranda, the man known as "Cap'n Webb" to most of the county, waved a hand to greet him.

As Jonathan got down from the buggy, Anthony grabbed the reins and led Nellie away. Across the barn lot, Jonathan spied another rig.

The pastor climbed the steps and the captain grasped his hand. "Thank you for coming, Preacher." His voice softened. "I think Mama may be leaving us this time."

They walked into the high-ceilinged hallway and mounted the winding staircase. As they entered the room where a small figure lay beneath a lacy coverlet, a memory sliced through Jonathan's heart. Just a year ago, he had entered the room where his beloved Kate lay dying. The pain grabbed at him, and he prayed for strength. He nodded to the doctor who was talking with Lucy Webb, the captain's wife, near the fireplace.

A chair stood beside the bed. The pastor sat and took the pale hand on the bedspread. He spoke softly. "Mrs. Webb, it's Jonathan Woolridge." No response.

Jonathan pulled out his worn black book and began to read, "The Lord is my Shepherd; I shall not want." A smile crept across the pale face and her eyelids fluttered open. After reading a few more verses, Jonathan touched the thin wrist searching for a pulse, and found none. Gently, he closed the withered eyelids.

Later, in the parlor, he was served coffee and sandwiches as he discussed plans for a funeral service with the Captain and his wife. Just as he rose to leave, a tall dark-haired woman came into the room.

"Mama," she said, going to Lucy's side, "Sophie is about to leave, and she's asked what we will need for tomorrow."

Jonathan stood dumbstruck. *Where did she come from? Why had he never seen this lovely person?*

Captain Webb spoke. "Preacher, I don't believe you've ever met my younger daughter Grace. She's been in Danville teaching. She just arrived home for the summer."

He must have held out his hand, because it was soon encased in a warmth that matched Grace's smile. "I'm so happy to meet you, Pastor. Mama and Papa have spoken highly of you. I'm looking forward to coming to your church, now that I'm back home."

"Yes," Jonathan mumbled. "I hope to see you there."

The captain walked Jonathan out to his buggy, which Anthony had brought around. "We'll have plenty of our people to help with the burial. She'll be laid to rest here in the family cemetery, of course, after the service in town."

Jonathan knew the story of how most of the Webbs' one hundred slaves had chosen to remain on the plantation after the Emancipation Proclamation, and John Webb had managed, with their help, to build the place back to a working farm after the War. Now, the second-generation plantation workers were share croppers on the land.

Twilight settled over the town as a weary Jonathan guided his horse into the stable. It was an ordinary day in the life of a pastor, but caring for the bereaved seemed to require much of his strength. Tomorrow he would join the Captain at the courthouse to help with legal papers, and the next day preach a funeral.

Louisa met him at the back door. He knew Nathaniel waited in the wagon, out in the alley. "Supper's in the warming oven, Preacher. The baby's fed and down for the night, and your mother is resting in her room."

"Thank you, Louisa," he said. Seeing the question in her eyes, he continued, "Mrs. Webb died this afternoon. Her funeral will be Friday morning at the Church. Would you tell Nathaniel, please?"

"Yes Sir, Preacher. I'm sorry for her passing, but she's been ailing for a long time. She be with Jesus now." Her voice carried a lilt of hope. "Goodnight, Preacher. Be sure you eat some supper," she said as she closed the door.

Seated at the table, Jonathan heard the rumble of the wagon. Restless, he rose, went outside and walked around the old church yard.

What was happening to him? He was a widower, still in mourning. Absently he rubbed his right hand, remembering the softness of a grasp, the light shining from hazel eyes, and the joy that settled over his heart when Grace Webb smiled at him.

Chapter 9

UNEXPECTED BLISS

The organist played softly, as mourners filed out of Oxford's First Presbyterian Church and gathered in small groups on the front steps and lawn.

"Well, Pastor, it was a real nice send-off for a great lady," said one of the elders, as he shook Jonathan's hand.

Susie Bullock, a cousin of the deceased, leaned close to the pastor. "Miss Mary *was* a great lady, but you and I know she was a bit opinionated." A mischievous smile shone through her tears.

Jonathan returned the smile. "Yes, she had her own ideas about how the church should be run."

Other parishioners, some dabbing at tears, gripped the pastor's hand as they left.

Jonathan made his way to the small parlor just off the Sanctuary where the family had gathered. He was doing what was expected, but he could not ignore the strange longing to see Grace's smiling eyes again.

Entering the room, he went to the Captain and Lucy, taking their hands in his. Both had tears in their eyes, but their smiles were warm. He shook hands with their son Joe, home from college for the service

"You'll come to the house for a little supper after the

43

graveside, won't you, Pastor?" Lucy asked.

Jonathan nodded, feeling Grace's eyes on him, "I'd be honored, Mrs. Webb."

The door opened, and Lester Parnel, the funeral home director, entered and stepped to Jonathan's side. "We'll be leaving as soon as you folks are ready," he said. "The hearse wagon is just outside, and another wagon full of flowers behind it." He shook his head slightly. "That lady was surely loved around here."

As the family filed out, Jonathan felt a touch on his arm. It burned through the coat's alpaca sleeve, right to his skin. He looked down, and Grace's eyes did that thing to his heart again. "Thank you, Pastor," she said, before climbing into the buggy with her parents, sister and two nieces.

"Nice work, Jonathan," said his friend Samuel, clapping him on the shoulder.

"We make a good team, my friend," answered Jonathan. "Next time *you* get the sermon." They laughed as they made their way to Jonathan's buggy.

Thirty minutes later, six strong, well-dressed men lowered the casket containing the body of the Webb matriarch into a freshly-dug grave in the family cemetery. Born on this land, Mary Bullock Webb was beloved for her charitable works and her strong spirit of fairness. As the mourners trailed off, the faint sound of keening was borne on the breeze.

At the big house, an abundant meal covered the long buffet in the dining room. Servants moved about, pouring coffee and water for guests who came to visit with the grieving family. The family's long-time butler spoke to some of the men, reminding them that "spirits" were available in the library.

Jonathan stood near the parlor door, speaking with members of his congregation. Lucy Webb approached and took his arm. "Excuse us, please. We want to be sure our pastor has a bite to eat before he leaves," she said, steering Jonathan toward the buffet.

And there she was again, smiling that disturbing smile. Grace hugged her sister Mary and placed a sisterly kiss on Samuel's cheek, but Jonathan was sure she looked straight at him.

A little later he made his way through the thinning crowd to the table where Grace was serving several kinds of cake.

She looked up at him. "And what would you like, Pastor Woolridge?" she asked.

He found he couldn't speak coherently. "It . . . doesn't matter," he managed.

"Then I'll give you some samples," she said placing three pieces of cake on a plate. Her laughter sounded to him like the tinkling of bells. "I'll ask May to bring you some coffee," she called, turning toward the kitchen. After a moment he realized he was expected to move on and find a place to sit.

Evening shadows fell across the porch, and servants lighted the parlor and dining room lamps, as Jonathan prepared to leave. He searched for the Webbs, and saw Grace attending her mother, who was seated on a brocade settee, with Joe. Just as he approached, she straightened up and smiled at him. He forgot what he had to say, but she spoke up.

"Thank you again, Pastor, for a beautiful service. It truly honored my grandmother." She paused, and looked into his eyes. "I do hope we'll be seeing you again soon."

"Oh yes, you must come out and have a look at the new pony I bought last week. Won't be long before that boy of yours will be ready to ride." The captain, having bid goodbye to some neighbors, arrived at his wife's side.

"Oh, Captain, James is only a year old," she said.

"Can't start 'em too young. Grace, you were no older than two when you sat your first horse."

"Captain, you exaggerate. She was led around the yard on old Princess, the gentlest pony we ever had," said his wife, laughing.

"Quite so, and now she's a talented horsewoman." He turned again to his pastor. "Jonathan, it would do you a world of good to come out and ride around these fields. Clears the mind."

"Thank you, Captain. I haven't ridden for pleasure in a long time."

The soft hand was on his arm again. "Perhaps, Monday afternoon would be a good time for you to have that pleasure," said Grace. "After preaching two sermons in two days, I would think you could use a little recreation."

He consulted a small black book. "I . . . have no plans for Monday afternoon," he said.

"Good," replied the captain, clapping him on the back. "Come for a brisk ride, and stay for supper."

"I look forward to it." Jonathan shook his friend's hand and turned toward the door. Grace was beside him. They were alone in the world. Her eyes looked into his as she said, "Goodbye, Pastor. We'll all be in our family pew tomorrow, and we'll look for you on Monday." The smile reached her beautiful eyes and he knew he had to get away, or he'd never get his mind on tomorrow's sermon.

𝕮𝖍𝖆𝖕𝖙𝖊𝖗 10

THE PROPOSAL

The late fall day was balmy. Sunshine burst through the study window and brightened the dark-paneled room where Jonathan sat making notes for Sunday's sermon.

He heard the front doorbell ring, and then Louisa's voice. "Morning. Come right on in."

The pastor strained to hear the response. "Thank you, Louisa. I brought a few sweet potatoes, and some winter squash. It's more than we can eat, and I thought you all might be able to use them."

"Yes Ma'am, Miss Grace. We're still enjoying those apples you brought us last week."

The voices began to fade, but he heard, "And how's my sweet boy this morning?" Laughter followed, and a high squeal from his son.

Jonathan lost interest in the sermon. He rose and went into the hall, where he unashamedly listened to the conversation from the kitchen.

"You know, Miss Grace, your Aunt Suzie come by here just last evening, brought us these turnips I'm cutting up. She told the preacher he needs a woman around here, to be a mama to his baby boy. She asked him had he thought about how you been working on the altar guild, and playing the piano, and how this child loves you." Louisa laughed merrily. "She had him blushing red as the apples in this here bowl."

"Oh, Louisa," Grace said with a sigh, "he hardly notices me, even when we're out riding on the farm. We rarely talk, and he seems in a hurry to get back to town, as soon as supper is over."

Louisa chuckled. "Seems to me he enjoys riding with you. Every Monday afternoon he asks me can I stay a little later and keep the baby for him to make a call. I know who he's calling on."

Jonathan made his way to the kitchen door. He saw Grace with little James on her lap, his hands held tightly in hers.

"Here's the way the lady goes . . . step, step, step," she sang, rocking gently. "And here's the way the gentleman goes . . . trot, trot, trot." She began juggling him on her knee. "And along comes the country boy . . . gallop-y, gallop-y, gallop-y, whee!" She bounced the happy child in the air and caught him close in her arms, both of them laughing.

"Good morning, Miss Webb," Jonathan said.

Grace caught her breath. "Good morning, Mr. Woolridge," she said, trying to control the wiggling boy in her arms, who was demanding, " Agin. Agin!"

"Uh . . . Louisa, would you have a cup of coffee handy?" He moved past the game which had started again.

"Sure enough, Preacher," Louisa wiped her hands on her apron, reached into the cabinet and took out two cups, with their saucers. After placing them on the table, she turned to pick up the coffee pot from the back of the stove.

Grace got up and put the child into his father's outstretched arms. "That horsey game wears me out, but he never seems to get enough." She sat at the table and took the steaming cup Louisa offered her.

Jonathan savored the nearness of his son. Soft blond curls tickled his neck as he held the child close. James settled on his father's lap, as Louisa handed Jonathan a small cup half full of milk.

"That big boy's drinking from a cup, now," she said, smiling at them both. "But be careful, Preacher." She handed him a dish towel. "Sometimes he spills more than he drinks." She picked up a wicker basket and said, "If you folks will excuse me, I need to get that wash on the line." She left through the back door, heading for the wash house.

Jonathan stroked his son's back awkwardly. Then he said, "Miss Webb, I hope you know how much I appreciate your coming by to play with James. His grandmother has little time—or patience—for him, and I ..."

Grace placed her cup in its saucer and studied a spot on the tablecloth, as heat flooded her cheeks.

Suddenly, Jonathan wanted to touch this lovely creature across the table from him.

At that moment James sat up, looked around the room, slid from his father's lap and scurried toward the door, calling, "Weesa, Weesa!"

Both Jonathan and Grace raced for him and almost collided, catching the child just as he pushed the door open.

Reaching around the wiggling body, Jonathan touched Grace's arm. He looked into those beautiful hazel eyes. "Grace," he said, calling her name for the first time, "we need you here. Do you know that?"

Grace took James and placed him in the play pen Nathaniel had fashioned for him, between the ice box and the pantry door. She took time to hand him a favorite toy before turning back to the pastor.

"I know," she said. "But, as much as I love being with this little boy, I can't keep coming here."

"Why?" He was suddenly fearful of the sadness in her voice.

"Because I'm leaving in a few weeks."

He felt a heavy weight land on his chest. "Leaving?"

She stepped closer to him. "Yes," she said. "The school where I taught last year has asked me to come back and finish out the year for a teacher who is getting married."

He sat down. "But why? You're needed here. Your parents.

. . we . . . James and I . . .” He was perspiring, and his hands felt clammy.

“I thought I was needed here. I mean here, at the manse, but you never mentioned anything until just now, and I don't even know whether it's just the boy who needs me, or . . .”

She turned and knelt by the play pen, kissing the child's soft head. Rising, she smiled at Jonathan. “I need to go. I promised Mama I'd stop by the market and the post office while I am in town.” She turned to leave, picking up a shawl from her chair.

In a trance, Jonathan watched her go. James began to whimper, and then to cry. He went to the play pen and picked up the boy. They started for the front door, just as it closed.

Then it hit him. She was truly leaving. He had to stop her. Racing through the front door, he shouted, “Miss Webb, Grace. Don't go!”

James was wailing now, and Louisa came around the porch and took him from his father's arms, disappearing into the house.

Grace turned toward him. “Why?”

“Because I . . . I . . . need you. No, I want you to stay.” She didn't move, and he walked to where she stood by the buggy.

“Oh, Grace, don't do this to us. Can't you see how much we need you?”

“We? You, or James?” She allowed herself, just for a moment, to look deep into his eyes.

“I . . . don't want to live without you. Please stay with us. Don't go away. We need you to . . .” For a man of words, he was rambling badly.

“Jonathan Woolridge, are you proposing, out here on the street?” Her laughter rippled across the morning air.

He adored her with his eyes. “I . . . suppose,” he said. “I've wanted to tell you for weeks now, but I thought you were just coming here because of James.”

“Tell me what?”

He shook his head. “Why . . . why . . .” A wagon rattled by, the driver waving at them, but he didn't notice. “Tell you that

I want you to stay with us, come here and live. It's obvious James needs a mother, and I need . . . someone too." He finished lamely, blushing hot above his celluloid collar.

She smiled up at him. "Then, Mr. Woolridge, my answer is 'yes.' I'll stay in Oxford and help you, but . . ."

"But what?" he asked, feeling the breath leave his body.

"We must be married in June, here at your church."

"I . . . I'll phone Samuel."

"He'll be delighted."

Chapter II

THE WEDDING
JUNE 15, 1904

Lucy Webb settled into the front pew and picked up her fan. The church was filled with summer flowers. It seemed the entire congregation had donated the beauty of their gardens. Candles glowed on the Communion table and a breeze whispered through the open windows. Joyful organ music echoed the gladness deep in Lucy's heart.

Across the aisle Elmira Woolridge was escorted to a seat by her son, Theodore, who then joined his brother at the front.

Suzie Bullock slipped into the second pew and leaned forward to speak to the mother of the bride. "The church hall is just beautiful. The ladies have outdone themselves with this reception. I know you'll be pleased."

Lucy turned and whispered, "This is a day the Captain and I thought would never come. Grace has been so particular about beaux, but it's obvious she is very much in love with our pastor. I do pray everything goes well for them today."

"I'm sure it will, but where are the other members of Mr. Woolridge's family? I thought he had several brothers."

"It seems Theodore is the only one who could arrange to come," Lucy said, her voice holding a tinge of resentment. "He is a very nice man. He came to our dinner last night, and he seems genuinely happy for his brother."

"Unlike his mother. Did you see her face, as she was seated?"

"Yes, well I believe she is having a difficult time accepting this marriage."

The organist swung into the Bridal Chorus from Lohengrin, and Suzie settled back into her pew. Down the aisle came the bride's sister Mary, in a floor-length pale green voile that accented her dark hair and eyes. She carried a bouquet, from her own garden, which matched the bride's flowers. Her young daughters preceded her, and were soon seated with their grandmother. Mary's smile overflowed with love and pride as she caught the eye of her husband in his black liturgical robe, standing with Jonathan at the front.

As if on signal, Lucy rose and turned, followed by the congregation. An audible gasp was heard, as the captain entered with a radiant bride on his arm. The dress, borrowed from her sister, sparkled with pearls, and its satin train flowed onto the aisle carpet. The veil, caught in her upswept hair with small white flowers, had been worn by both her mother and her sister.

Jonathan stood dumbstruck, not able to believe that this lovely creature approaching him was willing to be his bride. At the communion table they met, and the captain lifted Grace's small hand, and placed it in Jonathan's outstretched one, then took his place on the pew beside his wife.

At that moment, a shrill voice echoed from the church's balcony, "I wanta' go see," came between sobs, as Louisa carried the pastor's son out of the church.

Jonathan was never sure what his friend Samuel said, but suddenly, there was the benediction, and the proclamation, "I now pronounce you man and wife. What, therefore, God has joined together, let no man put asunder." They were walking back down the aisle to the jubilant cheers of his congregation.

Two hours later, Nathaniel pulled up to the church in the family buggy, and the couple were ushered into it for the ride to the railroad station. Grace tossed her bouquet to her eight-year-old niece, Elizabeth.

In their Pullman honeymoon car, Grace sat before a small dresser. Her wedding gown had been put away, and she was dressed in the soft, lacy white peignoir made with her own mother's loving hands. As she ran a brush through her long black hair, Jonathan, clad in pajamas, came to stand behind her.

Reverently, he lifted a strand of hair and brought it to his lips. Then he looked at her image in the mirror and said, "I still don't believe how blessed I am. You are a wonderful woman, to take on the life of a pastor's wife and the raising of a son."

Grace leaned into him and took his hand. "Mr. Woolridge, it's not the ministry, or even that adorable little boy I married. I married you."

He turned her around and pulled her into his arms.

She was surprised to feel the dampness of a tear on the face she kissed.

Chapter 12

CHANGE COMING

"Miss Grace, I just don't know how much more of this I can take." Louisa took a long pan from the oven, mopped her face with a towel and sat down.

Grace sat at the kitchen table beside five-year-old James, who was devouring a slice of warm bread. Melted butter ran down his chin and she grabbed a cloth to wipe it.

"Tell me about it, Louisa."

The graying head twisted. "Not in front of the child," she said.

"Mama-Grace," James said, around a mouthful of bread, "is Weesa gonna' cry?"

Grace took the boy on her lap. "No, Sweetie." She kissed his golden curls. "Not with you around."

To Louisa she said, "Tonight, just before Nathaniel comes to pick you up, we'll talk."

Then she looked at the boy. "Want to go and surprise your father?"

Soon after she moved into the manse, Grace turned the old study into a bright room where James not only played with blocks and trains, but where he sat for stories and art projects. Jonathan willingly moved his study to the old church parlor, where he said it was quieter, and more fitting for visits with parishioners.

Opening the front door, Grace heard a familiar voice from upstairs. "Louisa, fetch me some fresh water. This is not fit for bathing, let alone drinking, in this hot weather."

Grace and James followed the worn path to the church's side door. Holding the small hand, she felt a stab of sadness. Unbidden came the sharp memory of that stormy night six months ago, when they had frantically called the doctor, and her joy at carrying Jonathan's child was destroyed in a delirium of pain and loss. The tiny room that had been James' nursery remained closed, the crib untouched.

She knocked lightly on the study door, but James rushed right in. Jonathan turned from his desk and took off his spectacles as the boy flew into his arms. "Ride, Father!" he said, and around they went, in the old wooden swivel chair until Grace feared they might turn over. But her husband was laughing when they finally stopped, and it made her heart glad.

"Is it time for dinner?" he said, reaching for the watch in his vest pocket.

"In an hour or so. James finished his morning's work, so we came to surprise you."

"I wrote a story, Father," the boy crowed.

Grace laughed. "A very short one, which he told me, and I wrote it," she said. "But he has your gift for story-telling."

"Mama-Grace made bread for dinner," the boy said, sliding from his father's lap.

"Louisa is teaching me to cook, and today it was her wonderful salt-rising bread."

"It's good, Father. I had some already."

"Hot bread is bad for the digestion."

Grace reached for the child's hand. "James, let's walk around to the stable and see if Nathaniel needs you to help brush Nellie. Remember, he's taking us to the farm this afternoon."

The boy took Grace's hand. "Are you coming with us, Father?" he asked.

"Not today, James." He laid a hand on the boy's head. "I

have a sermon to write."

"Don't be late for dinner, Mr. Woolridge," Grace called as they walked out.

He stood at the door and watched them leave the church yard. *Why do I always say the wrong thing? She is the joy of my life, but today I saw the sadness in her eyes again.* He raised his own eyes to heaven. *Lord, I don't know what to do, to make her happy.*

Back at his desk, he stared at sermon notes until the telephone rang.

"Yes. I'll be right over," he told Henry Potter. The man's wife was dying, and they had no family.

Jonathan crossed the yard and stopped at the kitchen door. "Louisa, I may have to miss dinner. I'm on my way to the Potters."

"I understand, Preacher. Here, take Mr. Potter a loaf o' fresh bread." She grinned. "Your wife made it."

"She told me you're teaching her to cook. Thank you, Louisa."

"I'll keep your dinner warm, Preacher," she called, as he headed toward the stable.

It was early evening when Jonathan returned and found the two women in the kitchen. He had sat with his grieving parishioner until the man's wife was gone, and then stayed to make some arrangements for the burial. He was exhausted, as he began to eat. "Is James asleep already?" he asked.

"Yes, almost an hour ago," Grace answered. "He was tired from an afternoon of riding the pony and playing checkers with his grandfather. He could barely stay awake for a story and prayers."

Louisa went to the front hall and brought the pastor several pieces of mail. "The new postman brought these today, Preacher. I thought you'd like to see 'em before you go to bed."

Jonathan finished his meal, wiped his mouth on a napkin, and rose. "Thank you, Louisa," he said, taking the letters and turning toward the stairs.

Grace stood and reached up to kiss her husband's cheek. "I'll be up soon," she said. When he was gone, she turned to the faithful servant. "Now, tell me, Louisa."

The elderly black woman shook her head. "That woman just sit in her room all day, except when the church ladies come calling, and expects me to wait on her like I don't have nothing else to do."

She wiped a tear with the corner of her apron. "Missy, I don't mean no disrespect, but some days she just gets on my nerves. I been working at this Manse for a lot of years, and ain't nobody treat me like this. And the preacher, he don't notice none of it."

Grace placed a hand on Louisa's arm. "I know. She's not well, and I believe she's afraid of dying. Mr. Woolridge means to spend more time with his mother, but the church is growing and keeping him busier than ever." She sighed. "He hardly has time for James and me. Poor man, he's expected to be all things to all of us."

She looked into the brimming eyes. "But, Louisa, no one has cared for this family more than you have. Why, little James wouldn't be alive if it hadn't been for you. I don't know what we can do about Mrs. Woolridge. She's an unhappy lady, and has told me more than once that I don't live up to her expectations of a wife for her son. That's hard to take, but most of all, I want to please Mr. Woolridge and raise a happy, healthy boy, so I just try to be kind to her and not complain."

"Yes Ma'am. I try not to complain, but sometimes . . ."

Grace got up and put an arm around the thin shoulders. "I know, Louisa. I know. Just remember how much we love you, and depend on you."

The door opened and Nathaniel stepped in. "I'm ready," Louisa said. "See you in the morning, Missy." She smiled as she followed her husband out.

Picking up the lamp from the table, Grace was headed toward the stairs when she heard her husband's voice, "Grace! Come here, quickly!"

Chapter 13

AN OPEN SECRET

Grace heard the urgency in her husband's voice and hurried up the stairs.

He was standing in the door to their bedroom holding a letter, and grinning.

"It's from the First Presbyterian Church in Wilson," he said. "When we were all at Stem for James' birthday party last month, Samuel mentioned they were ready to call a pastor, but I never gave it another thought. Why would they consider me?" His voice held an edge of wonder. "It's a big, city church. Why, they even have a church staff!"

She laughed as she joined him. He handed her the letter from the Wilson church's clerk of Session.

"Looks like my brother-in-law highly recommended you," she said, with pride in her voice. She studied the letter. "So that's where those people were from. Remember the two ladies and a man who showed up three Sundays ago? In our congregation they stood out like rank strangers, and they hurried off before any of us could speak to them. Cousin Suzie mentioned they might be a pulpit committee."

They sat on the window seat. "Do you know what this means?" he asked.

"Yes, no more rushing to get the bulletin together and to the printer by Friday noon. You'll have a secretary for that, and for answering the letters you labor over, and the files scattered around your office. You might even have reasonable hours." She chuckled. "You won't be expected to pastor the whole town and countryside, Presbyterian or not."

"Wilson is a long ways from Stem," he said softly.

She reached for his hand. "I know," she said. "I'm trying not to think of that." She rose and walked to the fireplace. "I've never been far away from Mama and Papa, except for a few months of school and the year I taught." She sighed. "And now they're getting older. Mama's arthritis sometimes keeps her in bed for most of the day. It means so much when James and I go for a visit."

"The Captain tells me the boy is becoming quite a horseman. They're very fond of our son."

"He's the shining light of their lives these days."

He came to stand beside her. "Would it be difficult for you, Grace, to be far away from your family?"

She hesitated, then nodded, "Yes. Yes, Mr. Woolridge, it would." She turned to face him. "But you are my husband, and if God is calling you to that church in Wilson, then James and I will be happy there."

He took her in his arms. "You are God's gift to me," he said, "and I promise that the two of you will have a long visit to the farm every summer."

"That will console the adoring grandparents."

He walked to the bed and sat, heaving a sigh. "Oh, Grace. We haven't even prayed about this. We don't know what God's will is in this matter."

"No, we don't, but I can see the excitement in your eyes. You've served faithfully here for five years, and it just may be time for a change." She sat beside him. "Jonathan Woolridge, you are a powerful preacher, and a devoted pastor. Perhaps God will reward your service with a prosperous congregation who will appreciate your gifts."

He shook his head. "I just never dreamed . . ."

"Well I did. The people here expect too much of you, and it doesn't help that your wife is kin to most of them. That church could be a new start for you, and for our family."

"I have been feeling restless of late. I've caught myself day-dreaming at times, about what I'm supposed to do for the rest of my life and ministry."

He went to the desk and laid the letter down. "Grace, we may be getting ahead of ourselves. There are a few ecclesiastical hoops we need to jump through, and the wheels of Presbytery move slowly."

"I will join you in prayer. Goodness knows I have mixed emotions about this whole thing." She smiled. "How long do you think we can keep it to ourselves?"

"No one knows but the two of us."

"Mr. Woolridge, Oxford is a very small town, and the preacher's business is everybody's business. Somehow it will leak out, you mark my words."

"Still," he said. "it's far from settled. I wouldn't start packing yet."

Chapter 14

AUCTIONEERS AND GROWING PAINS

Jonathan replaced the telephone receiver on its hook and turned to his cluttered desk. He had been in Wilson less than a week, and already felt overwhelmed by new responsibilities. And just now, Jack Davenport called to say that Edna Singleton, the church's secretary, for thirty years, had resigned.

How was he going to maneuver through this labyrinth that was his new charge?

He took out his watch. Almost dinner time. Perhaps he would walk over to the manse and see how Grace was doing with the unpacking.

"I'm out here, Mr. Woolridge," Grace answered, as he entered the house and called her name.

In the kitchen, Grace and a large, sterned-faced, woman were pulling newspaper-wrapped packages of china and utensils from a barrel.

"Oh look, Mattie. Here's my teakettle," said Grace. "Since we already found the cups, we could make tea."

The other woman nodded. "If we just knew where the tea got to, we could, yes Ma'am." She went on unwrapping and setting out dishes to wash, never changing the grim expression on her dusky features.

"Good morning, ladies. I see you are making progress. I was

wondering about dinner." Jonathan looked at the table covered with cooking pots and dishes.

"Oh, Mr. Woolridge" said Grace, coming around the table to greet him. "As soon as we finish this barrel, so Isaiah can take it to the storehouse, we'll be eating in the dining room."

"But I don't see . . ."

"Father," piped up a small voice as the screen door opened and slammed, "I found a swing in the back yard. A boy like me lived here before."

The pastor looked at his son. "Have you been out there alone? You don't know your way around yet. You could get lost."

"Mr. Isaiah was with me. He showed me the swing, and a big old wagon he says we can hitch to Nellie when we go to town to watch the 'baccer wagons come in."

"What are you talking about? What are 'baccer wagons?" Jonathan asked.

Grace laughed and bent to give James a hug.

"Preacher," said Mattie, sighing audibly. "Those 'baccer wagons come in every year about this time, bringing leaves to market at the warehouses downtown."

"Yes, Father, and they have auc-tion-eers that sing funny songs—Mr. Isaiah can do it just like they do—and sell the 'baccer to big, im-por-tant men."

Jonathan pulled out a chair, emptied it of crumpled paper and sat down. "For a five-year-old boy who just moved here three days ago, you surely have learned a lot about what goes on in this city." He smiled and pulled James onto his lap.

Grace, coming up from the depths of the barrel with a wrapped package, gave a whoop. "Mattie, here it is! Mama's Haviland soup tureen. Oh, I hope it's not damaged like the teapot was." Quickly she unwrapped the large piece of china and, making a place on the table, set it down. "Isn't it beautiful? I can't wait until the weather's cool enough to fill it with good hot vegetable soup."

"Yes Ma'am, but right now we need to fix these gentlemen

some of that good food Miss Davenport brought this morning."

"You're right, Mattie. I expect they're starving. Anyway, we got the last barrel emptied. Hallelujah!"

"Yes Ma'am. I'll call Isaiah to come get it, and then I'll put some water on to heat so I can wash all these things and put them away."

"Let's find some plates we can rinse off. You and Isaiah must take some time to eat as well."

"Will Miss Elmira be eating with us, you think?"

"I asked her earlier, and she says she'd like a plate in her room. She seems tired from the move."

"Yes Ma'am. I'll take it up to her." As she washed the plates, Mattie mumbled to herself, "Don't know what she's so tired from. Ain't done a lick of work around here."

Soon the family of three was seated at the large dining room table. Grace dished out tantalizing helpings of meatloaf and potatoes, green beans and stewed tomatoes, while Mattie brought glasses of iced tea, and a cup of milk for James.

As was the family custom, they held hands and Jonathan asked God's blessing on the food they were about to receive.

"Mr. Woolridge, all this bounty came from the Davenports. Isn't he the clerk of Session?"

"Yes, and already I'm coming to rely heavily on his judgment in many things. Do you have any idea how many committees this church has? There are committees for the women, for the Session, committees for the Sunday School, and this morning, Silas Johnson called about a committee for cleaning and maintaining the church and grounds."

"Isn't that part of Isaiah's job, as sexton?" Grace took a long drink of tea.

"Of course, but Silas is chairman of the Deacons and owns the feed and grain store in town. He wants to plant grass around the entrance."

"What's wrong with that? Seems very nice to me."

"Yes, it does to me too, except that the Ladies' Auxiliary wants to plant flowers in the same area." His voice became almost strident.

"Oh yes, Mrs. Littleton invited me to a beautification committee meeting at her house tomorrow afternoon."

Jonathan groaned. "Another committee. And what am I to tell Silas?"

"I'm sure you'll handle that with wisdom and gentleness." Grace smiled as she began to dish up the apple pie.

"Pie, Mama-Grace," squealed James. "Look, I ate all my dinner."

"Why yes, you did, young man. Here is your dessert."

While James was busy with his pie, Grace asked, "Mr. Woolridge, have you met your secretary? I heard she was new to the job."

"You knew . . . how did you . . .?" Jonathan stuttered.

Grace forked up a bite of pie. "Mattie's cousin works for Miss Singleton's mother. It seems the lady thinks it's time to retire."

"Retire? When I desperately need a competent secretary?"

"I believe she was heard to comment that she wasn't up to 'breaking in' another preacher." Grace began to laugh.

"How can she say that? I *need* 'breaking in.' Jack said he was bringing a young lady by the office this afternoon. I think she's his wife's cousin. Probably has no secretarial experience whatsoever."

Grace smiled. "I'm sure she will be competent, and you will be able to teach her your routine." She became pensive, "But I do hope she'll be able to grasp the importance of caring for members of the congregation."

"I thought that was my job."

"No, Mr. Woolridge. Your job is to preach, counsel, visit the sick, hold funerals, baptize babies and celebrate weddings."

"That's simple enough, but you haven't seen my desk."

"I will pray the secretary can take care of that, as well as taking shorthand, typing and screening the people who come by the office."

"Sounds good to me." Rising from the table, Jonathan

looked at his son, who was finishing his pie. "James, what will you do this afternoon?"

"Me and Mr. Isaiah . . ." He stole a glance at his mother and corrected himself. "Mr. Isaiah and I are gonna' put the barrels away in the storeroom and hitch up the old wagon for our ride downtown."

Grace placed a hand on the child's shoulder. "First, you'll have a little nap." When she saw the small face begin to screw into a frown, she added, "After a story, of course."

Chapter 15

SAD HEART, BRAVE WORDS

A small breeze stirred the curtains as an electric fan whirred in the parlor of the manse. Grace and her sister Mary sat enjoying frosty glasses of lemonade. A plate of sugar cookies rested on the marble-top table between them.

"I do believe summer is hotter and longer, here in Wilson, than it was in Oxford," Grace said, "I had hoped September would be more bearable."

"The hot summers are one reason Samuel and I are considering the General Assembly's offer of building lots at the new conference center, up near Asheville," Mary said, sipping her lemonade. "It seems the Church wants to establish a summer retreat for pastors and missionaries." She put her glass on the table. "They're calling it 'Montreat'. Isn't that a lovely name? The cost seems reasonable, and there will be training conferences each summer, with programs for the children."

Grace shifted in her chair. "Mr. Woolridge mentioned that some months ago, but I told him I really didn't see how we could afford it, and we spend much of the summer at the farm."

Mary nodded. "I understand. Summers are always good at Stem." She laughed. "We had some good growing-up times there, didn't we? I'm so glad James can enjoy it too, just like my girls always have."

Grace looked away for a moment. "Yes, he had a wonderful time this year, especially learning to ride his own pony. Of course, I believe his grandfather enjoyed it even more."

Mary laughed. "Papa is certainly proud of that little boy. He's brought a great deal of joy to both of them." She reached for her glass again. "We simply must get these cousins together more often."

Grace sighed. "I hated to leave this time. Mama and Papa suddenly seem to be much older, with Mama's arthritis and Papa's old war wound acting up." She looked up and smiled at her sister. "Mama was looking forward to another visit with the girls."

"Samuel had a two-day Presbytery meeting in Oxford, so he took the girls up for a visit before school starts. I planned to get a lot of housework done, without them underfoot, but I got tired of cleaning closets, and decided to come and see my sister." She laughed and lifted a cookie from the rose-covered china plate. "Mama is teaching the girls to do some lovely handwork, even though I'm sure it makes the pain in her fingers worse." She bit into the cookie. "You have an excellent cook."

Grace smiled. "Yes, she is very good, for all her grumbling about how hard she works."

Mary laughed. "Well, I believe Louisa spoiled you."

"You're right. She was a rare treasure, and suffered through a good deal with this family. Little James . . ." She looked up and smiled at a skinny figure waiting in the doorway. "Come in, James," she said, reaching her hand to him. "Let Aunt Mary see how you've grown since her last visit."

Immediately, the child bounced into the room and headed straight for the outstretched arms of his beloved aunt. He seated himself on a chair and said, "Aunt Mary, did you know that big cigarette companies buy their tobacco here in Wilson?"

"Oh my, what a vocabulary for a seven-year-old boy," she answered. "Well, yes, I think I did know that."

"Sometimes Mr. Isaiah takes me to the warehouse and I get

to listen to the auctioneers." He giggled. "They're funny singing their songs. And there's a big statue on the square, with a man riding a horse, but it's an awful big horse. My pony won't ever be that big."

"You're learning a lot about your new home, James. I'm glad you have a friend like Mr. Isaiah."

"Yes Ma'am, and I have another friend." He stood up. "His name is James too, but his mama calls him Jimmy. He comes over to play on the swing in our back yard, and he even has a sack full of marbles."

Both ladies laughed, and Mary said, "I'm sure you and Jimmy have some good times together."

"Yes Ma'am and I gotta' go now, 'cause Mr. Isaiah's waiting for me." He looked at Grace. "May I be excused?"

She nodded and he scooted out of the room.

"My, what a little man," said Mary. "You and Jonathan are doing a fine job with him." She took another sip of her drink.

Grace sighed. "I'm afraid, Mr. Woolridge doesn't spend much time with his little boy."

Mary put her glass down. "Do I hear a hint of sadness in my sister's voice?"

"Oh, Mary." Grace forced a smile. "He's just so busy. He's been invited to serve on the town board, and the church is more and more demanding. I had hoped . . ." she blinked away tears.

Mary laid a hand on her arm. "Oh, Grace. I had no idea there was any problem. Samuel is so pleased with how the church is growing, and we keep hearing how much the people love their pastor."

Grace nodded, blinking back tears. "Yes, they do love him, and I'm happy about that. He seems to revel in the work, and I think his preaching is better than ever. He's such a good man, and a good pastor."

"So why the tears?"

"Oh, I know I'm being impatient and ungrateful, but I miss him. When we were first married, we seemed to grow closer every day, until I lost the baby. I think that's when he began to shut us away," she said, wiping her tears with the dainty napkin. "And he and I are . . . not close anymore."

"Oh, you poor dear. I had no idea."

Grace shook her head. "I think he never properly grieved for Kate. He kept his sadness put away in a box somewhere, and now, every time he looks at James, I see it . . . the pain. Do you realize how very much the child resembles his mother? I believe it stabs his father's heart, sometimes." She stopped to dab at her eyes again. "It hurts me to see how much James adores his father, and how Mr. Woolridge is less and less able to show him affection."

Mary reached out and took her sister's hand. "I'll be praying for you, my dear. I know you love him dearly, and I'm sure he loves you, and that precious little boy."

"Please, Sister, don't mention this to Samuel. He and Mr. Woolridge are good friends, and while I wish he would confide in Samuel, I'm afraid he won't talk with anyone. Heaven knows, I've tried."

"But, my dear, if Samuel and I could pray together for the two of you . . ."

"No! Mr. Woolridge must never know I've confided in you about this. It is all too personal."

Chapter 16

GROWING UP, HEARING GOD'S CALL

"Mama-Grace, have you seen my notebook?"

Grace felt a pang of sadness at the maturity in her son's voice. Where was the little boy who brought so much delight with his quick hugs and giggles? What happened to the years between a curious toddler and this tall, lanky nine-year-old who always seemed to have his head in a book?

"I believe it's on the hall table, James," she called from the kitchen where she was preparing her husband's breakfast. James flew through the kitchen, kissed her cheek, and was out the door. A moment later she watched him hop on his bicycle, headed for school.

She was just breaking an egg into the hot pan when the pastor walked in. "Good morning, Grace," he said. He was dressed for the day, in his black alpaca suit, stiff collar and string tie.

She set the platter of sausage and eggs on the table, poured coffee into two cups, and sat opposite him, bowing her head as Jonathan led them in a morning prayer.

Spooning food onto his plate, he asked absently, "The boy get off to school already?"

She helped herself to the food and answered, "Yes, he seemed a bit hurried this morning, would hardly touch his oatmeal. I worry that he's too serious about school."

"Nonsense, he's discovering the joy of learning. He's always been a thoughtful one."

"Yes, he does have an insatiable desire to discover all he can." She turned toward her husband. "Mr. Woolridge, did you know that he is thinking of going into the ministry?"

He looked up, startled. "At such a young age? How can he perceive a call to the ministry?"

She smiled as she stirred her coffee and took a sip before answering. "He adores his father, you know."

Johnathan began to squirm in his chair. "That's no reason for such a decision." He took a long drink of coffee and looked at her thoughtfully. "Why do you say that?"

"It's true. He always has, since he could toddle after you around the house. Don't you remember how he would sneak into your study with his book, even before he could read, just to sit with you?"

Jonathan chuckled. "I was always surprised to find him there. Sometimes he had fallen asleep by the time I was ready to leave."

"And now he wants to follow in your footsteps," Grace said, rising to gather up the dishes and carry them to the sink.

The pastor put his napkin in its silver ring and shook his head. "I must find time to talk with him. The ministry is a serious calling, and must be from God Himself."

"I know," she said, tying on her large white apron, "and I think he knows that too. After all, he's sat under the preaching of a true servant of God all his life."

"Humph," was all he could muster, as he turned and went down the hall.

She was running hot water into a dishpan when the back door opened, letting in a chilly breeze. Mattie's voice was reproachful. "Now, Missy, you get your hands out of that dishwater. You want the ladies beautification committee to think you don't have no good help around here?"

Grace obeyed, wiping her hands on the apron she lifted over her head. "I certainly don't mind washing a few dishes,

Mattie," she said with a chuckle. "What I do mind is listening to the same arguments over and over about where to plant pansies in the church yard."

Mattie's gruff voice came from the sink. "Well, I can't do that for you, but I can finish up here and get the washing started before I take some breakfast up to Miss Elmira."

"Thanks, Mattie. I'll run up and see how my mother-in-law is feeling this morning. She'll be ready for her breakfast soon, I expect, and she thinks no one can fix it but you."

Climbing the steps, Grace paused as she heard voices coming from the bedroom at the head of the stairs.

"Mother, this is the day the Lord has made. You need to get up and enjoy it."

"Oh, Son, my arthritis is worse this morning. I hardly slept for the pain. I may take my pill, and have a little nap after Mattie brings my breakfast."

"Mother, you know she's not your personal maid. She has the whole household to look after."

"But I need help getting around, and you and Grace are always so busy."

"I have a meeting just after dinner today, and then I promise to take you out for a ride in the buggy. We can make a call at the Brierley's. You know they recently lost Mr. Brierley's father, and I haven't been by to visit since the funeral. You will enjoy the ride, this beautiful autumn day."

Grace watched as the older woman reached out a trembling hand and touched Jonathan's arm. "You are such a good son, but I don't want to be any trouble to you."

"Nonsense, Mother. You make sure to dress warmly for the ride, and I'll be home about three. Perhaps James would like to go with us."

"That child is too rambunctious," she said, but she smiled as she spoke.

Minutes later, at the door to the church office, Jonathan was greeted by his secretary, Evangeline Spruill. "Morning, Preacher. Busy day today. Some things on your desk."

She was efficient, and wasted no breath on small talk. Evangeline was one of the town's "unclaimed blessings," and lived with her widowed mother a few blocks from the church.

Entering his office, he heard the telephone ring.

"Morning, Mrs. Johnson," he heard his secretary's crisp greeting.

He stood by the door for a moment and listened.

"No, Ma'am. The Preacher is busy this morning, getting ready for a Presbytery Committee meeting. 'Fraid he can't see you today."

After a pause, she said, "I'll tell him, Mrs. Johnson. Sorry about your lumbago," and she hung up. The pastor smiled and went to his desk. Over the years, he had come to appreciate his secretary's brusque manner, which saved him many hours and much frustration.

On his desk lay the morning's mail and a few notes in Evangeline's tight handwriting. He picked up one envelope with a return address he didn't recognize. The postmark read, "Cornelius, North Carolina."

Chapter 17

ONE MORE MOVE
1910

Grace Woolridge turned around in the middle of her new home's living room and let out a heavy sigh. Where was she going to put the stately furniture they had brought from Wilson? This house located next door to Cornelius First Presbyterian Church, was a small bungalow compared with the antebellum-style manse she had lived in for the past four years.

"God surely knew what he was doing when He took Grandma Woolridge on Home, before we left Wilson," she thought. "This house is barely large enough for the three of us." She remembered the funeral, just three months ago, when it seemed the whole town turned out to show respect for their pastor's mother—and for their pastor. "He was beloved in that town," she thought, with gratitude. "But with the growth of the town and the church, and so many changes, it was time for a move." She slipped into a prayer. *Lord, please help my husband to see Your hand here, and to see how he can serve you, even in this small town.* She sighed. *We're not getting any younger. Sometimes, when I catch him dozing in the afternoon, I worry about his health.*

A knock on the door interrupted her ruminations, and she discovered two large overalled men at her door. "Where you want this furniture, Ma'am?" one of them asked, holding his hat in his hand.

She looked up and smiled. "Let me come to the truck and see what we can do," she said, still wondering where they would put everything.

As the men worked, she directed the placement of a large drop-leaf table, the arm chair and side chairs and a comfortable couch, all into the front parlor. It was not spacious, but the furniture fit, and it looked comfortable when they finished. Then, she watched as they brought in the large dining room table, the high china closet and massive cherry sideboard. After climbing the stairs with bed rails, mattresses and springs. they began the unloading of endless boxes containing the pastor's books.

Huffing under the load, one of the men asked, "Ma'am, do the preacher read all these books?"

"Yes, believe it or not, he does, "Grace answered, laughing.

While the men unpacked books under Jonathan's direction, Grace made the beds, digging into chests and trunks for sheets, pillow cases and towels. Later she headed down to the kitchen to prepare some lemonade for the workers.

After a few minutes, she heard a knock on the back door.

"Hello," she said, going to open the door. "I'm Mrs. Woolridge. Won't you come in?"

A tall, heavy-set lady balancing a large platter covered with a tea towel entered. "Just wanted to welcome our new preacher's family," she said, setting the food on the table. "I'm Janie Brown, and my sister Geraldine Simpson will be along later, with the rest of the meal."

"How lovely of you both," said Grace, glancing at the platter of ham surrounded by deviled eggs. "Won't you sit down? I'm about to prepare some lemonade for the movers, and then we can visit."

"Oh no, not today. You are far too busy. I'll be by again tomorrow." She stepped to the door and called, "Millie, come on in, dear."

Grace watched as a tall, shy girl quietly entered, carrying a covered cake plate.

Janie took the cake and placed it on the table. "Mrs. Woolridge, this young woman is very good at washing dishes and cleaning floors. Since the Manse has no 'help', I'm lending her to you for the next few days, until you can get unpacked and settled." She smiled at the girl, whose eyes studied the floor. "Her mother has worked for our family since before Millie was born, and I can recommend her work highly."

At that she turned, opened the door, and left.

Grace took a deep breath. "Well, Millie, you are a Godsend," she said, reaching into a barrel and extracting two glasses. "You can start by washing these glasses, while I prepare refreshment for the men working in the study."

"Yes Ma'am, Miss Woolridge," the girl said, barely above a whisper.

"Now, Millie, we've got a lot of work to do, you and I. As soon as I have taken this tray up to the movers, we'll get all these barrels unpacked, the dishes washed, and those cabinets filled. By the end of the day, the place will look like home."

As she filled the glasses and put them on a tray, she asked, "How old are you, Millie?"

"Seventeen, Ma'am." Millie swished more glasses in hot sudsy water and then rinsed them.

"Are you married, Millie?" Grace continued, beginning to slice the cake.

"No Ma'am," she sighed, then brightened, "but I got me a baby boy."

"Oh," said Grace, preparing to leave the kitchen—and the conversation. "I . . . I hope you'll bring him by to meet us."

Millie turned, hands still in the dishwater, "Miss Woolridge?" she said, alarm in her voice.

"Yes, Millie?"

"I hope you ain't planning to feed all that cake to those men. Miss Brown makes the lightest angel food cake in the county, wins ribbons all the time at the fair."

Grace laughed. "No, Millie. I'll save some for my men to enjoy."

By noon the house was beginning to look like home, with rugs on the dark floors and a vase of flowers from the yard gracing the dining room table.

James, who had been out on his bicycle exploring the small town, came into the kitchen and immediately noticed the cake, "Man, that looks good, and am I hungry."

"James, this young lady working so hard at the sink is named Millie. Millie, this is my son James."

"Hey, Miss Millie," James said, "I'm sure glad you're here. Mama Grace would have *me* washing dishes, and I've got some more exploring to do around here."

Grace shook her head at her son's exuberance. "Sit down and have some dinner before you try the cake," she said, sliding a plate of sliced bread and the platter of ham toward the hungry 10-year-old. She turned to fill a bowl with beans from a pot on the stove, and took it to him. "Want some lemonade?" she asked.

"Yes' Ma'am," he said, his mouth already full. The boy concentrated on eating for a few minutes and then said, "Mama-Grace, wait till you see downtown. There's only one street with about five stores! Nothing like Wilson."

Another knock on the door sent Grace to meet the promised sister. Opening the door wide, she greeted a lady bearing a large pot covered with a towel.

"Come in," she said, "you must be Mrs. Brown's sister."

Heaving a sigh, the lady set the pot on the table. "She always beats me to the new preacher," she said. Then she smiled, holding out a hand. "I'm Geraldine Simpson," she said, "We're so glad you're here."

Grace took the slim, cool hand. "Thank you, Mrs. Simpson. You and your sister are very kind, and you can see that your gifts are appreciated," she said, turning to James, who quickly remembered his manners, wiped his mouth and rose to greet the company.

"This is my son James," Grace said. "James, these dear ladies have brought us a wonderful meal."

Swallowing a mouthful of bread, James nodded. "Thank you Ma'am."

"Won't you come into the parlor for a visit?" Grace asked.

"Only for a moment," her guest answered. "I must get back to the office."

Seated in the front room, Grace asked. "Do you work here in town, Mrs. Simpson?"

"Yes," Geraldine answered. "I'm a receptionist, for Dr. Sloan. I'm sure you'll get to know him." She looked a little flustered, and added, "Though not because of any serious maladies, I hope." She twisted a lace handkerchief and managed an embarrassed laugh. "And, by the way, I am MISS Simpson. Janie and I grew up here in Cornelius. Our father owned a thousand acres of land and had share croppers who raised the cotton and tobacco." She sighed and shook her head, becoming suddenly sad. "But those days are gone. Papa sold all but a few hundred acres to developers, so people can live here and work in Charlotte. The share croppers have all left, looking for a better life up north, I suppose."

Grace laid a sympathetic hand on the lady's arm, and she looked up, forcing a bright smile. "But life goes on. I live with Janie and her husband. Their two sons finished at Davidson College and moved away, so it's just the three of us left in Papa's big old house."

As the lady rose to leave Grace asked, "Is Davidson a large college?"

"Oh, my dear, yes," answered Geraldine. "It's very well known in Presbyterian circles, and of course, it's only a few miles from here." She glanced toward the kitchen. "Perhaps one day your own son will study there."

Closing the etched-glass front door, Grace headed again for the kitchen where a lively discussion was going on. James had many questions about his new home town, and Millie had the answers.

"Where do you and your family live?" he wanted to know.

Millie dried her hands on a tea towel and began putting dishes into the cabinets. "Across the tracks. White folks round here call it 'Niggertown,' but it's got a real name, Beaulaville, after the A. M. E. Zion church there."

"Could I come to your church sometime?"

"I dunno', Mister James. I ain't never seen no white folks there."

"Why? Don't you worship God there too?"

"Sure we do, but I guess we do it different, or something." She shrugged her thin shoulders. "That's just how it is." She heard Grace's footsteps and hurriedly turned back to the sink.

"Great work, Millie," said Grace. "Now, James, before you take off again on that bicycle, I want you to get this empty barrel into the storehouse out back. Perhaps Millie can help you get it out the door and then you can roll it across the back yard."

"Yes Ma'am, Mama-Grace," the boy said. "I sure do miss Mr. Isaiah."

She laughed. "I'm sure you do. But he taught you well."

Grace heard the front door open, and she greeted her husband as he entered the kitchen. "Good afternoon, Mr. Woolridge. I'm so glad you could get away from the church long enough to have a little dinner. The sisters Simpson have brought some delicious ham and vegetables, to say nothing of an award-winning angel food cake."

"Just a little lemonade and a sandwich, please Grace. I need to make some calls this afternoon." He pulled a list from his pocket, as he sat down. "We have several rather needy families in the church, and they have been without a pastor for almost two years now."

"But Mr. Woolridge, we just got here. Can't the visits wait until tomorrow?"

"I have a busy schedule in the office tomorrow, and people expect the pastor to visit in the afternoon. You know that, Grace."

"Father, may I go with you? You said I'm getting good at driving the team," James said, from the doorway.

"That would be helpful, James. I could study my sermon notes as we ride." He glanced at Grace and continued, "That is, unless your mother needs you here."

The boy looked at his step-mother, who smiled and patted his hand. "As soon as you take care of this barrel, you go with your father, James. Millie and I will finish here. By suppertime you won't recognize the place."

Chapter 18

A FESTIVE NOTION

A cold wind whipped the barren trees and brought a gust of chilly air into the kitchen as Millie struggled to drag two tubs from the porch. Grace began filling them with a hose attached to the kitchen sink faucet. "We'll have to hang these clothes in the dining room again, Millie," she said. "It seems winter is truly here, with all these cold, rainy days."

"Yes Ma'am." Millie's hands were busy pulling sheets from a wicker basket and loading them into the washing machine, already churning with soapy water, which Grace had filled earlier. The tubs with rinse water stood on benches nearby. "That furnace gonna' dry these clothes before the day's over, I expect."

"It was good of Mr. McCullough to run clotheslines in the dining room for us. I don't know what we'd do without that, in the winter." Grace laughed as she folded a wet sheet and carefully fed it between the rollers into the first rinse tub. "Mr. Woolridge is very good at explaining the Scriptures, but he's not much of a handyman."

"Mister James said he made that rocking chair in the parlor," Millie remarked.

"Yes, he has inherited his family's gift for woodworking." Grace smiled as she lifted a basket, heavy with wet clothes.

"He does beautiful work, and it seems to help get his mind off the church's problems. Sometimes, I think he works out his sermons there in the barn with those tools."

As soon as the wash was finished and draped across the makeshift clotheslines, Grace pulled out her dough tray. "Millie, while you put clean sheets on the beds, I'm going to start the week's baking. With the Women's Auxiliary Christmas luncheon this week, I won't have much time later."

Millie emptied the tubs into the sink, wiped them dry and took them to the back porch. She returned to roll the washing machine into a corner of the kitchen. "I know you like to have some of your fresh hot bread for Mister James when he comes in from school and work." She hid a grin.

Grace was opening the kitchen cabinet which contained flour, and a built-in sifter. "You know me well, Millie. I do enjoy feeding that boy! He has a long walk from town, and I worry about him in this weather." She glanced toward the window, where rain was beginning to spatter the panes. She put a large, brown crockery bowl under the sifter and began to turn the handle.

It was nearly dark when she heard the back-door slam.

"Mama-Grace, I'm home. Sure smells good in here!"

"First, you get out of those wet clothes," Grace said, as she came into the kitchen. "Take those muddy boots to the porch, and hang your coat over a chair in the dining room."

He grinned, unloading an armful of books and shucking the heavy coat at the same time. He sat down and pulled off heavy boots, then took them to the porch.

"It's December, all right," he said, closing the door against a gust of wind. "Mmmm! Sticky buns!"

"Want some coffee with them?" she asked.

"No Ma'am, I'll get a glass of milk." He came around the table, gave her a hug and kissed her cheek. "You know how to warm a fellow's heart, Mama-Grace."

She blushed and patted his hand. "Eat up, now, before they get cold. And no more than two. You don't want to spoil your supper."

James munched thoughtfully, while she poured herself a cup of coffee and joined him at the table.

"Mama-Grace, do you think we could have a Christmas tree this year? At school today, Simon was talking about going out to Mr. McCullough's farm and cutting a tree for their family." He took a big bite, chewed, washed it down with a swig of milk and went on, "Made me think. We've never had a Christmas tree."

A look of sadness darkened his step-mother's face. "That's something you'll have to talk with your father about."

"But didn't you ever want a tree? I remember going to Grandpa Webb's house, when I was little, and they had that great big tree in the parlor. It was like something magic, with all the candles on it."

"Yes, Son. We always had a big tree at Mount Welcome." A faraway look came into her eyes. "We'd take the sleigh, go deep into the woods and select the best one to bring back and set up in the parlor. Your Aunt Mary and I would decorate it with keepsakes and things we made, like popcorn strings and pictures. Mama added the candles, each one clipped to the tip of a limb. Our parents always lighted them on Christmas Eve, after we got home from church."

James watched with amusement as his step-mother seemed to travel far away, to a time of remembered wonder.

Suddenly she put her hands on the table and stood up. "You need to bring in a load of wood for the fireplace, James, and I need to get supper ready."

When he stood, she said softly, "We'll talk about this at supper, but I don't want you to get your hopes up about a tree."

Later as the little family sat around the kitchen table, Grace ladled out bowls of steaming potato soup. A basket of fresh-baked bread was nearby.

"James, would you offer the blessing for our meal?" Jonathan asked.

"Lord, we thank You for taking care of us today, and for this good food, especially the bread Mama-Grace baked for us. Amen"

Grace picked up the basket. "James already had some sticky buns," she said, "but I managed to save a few for tomorrow's breakfast."

"Grace, you know hot bread is not good for the digestion," Jonathan said.

"Yes, I remember that, and I have a loaf from the first batch for you. It's cold already." A smile lit her eyes as she handed him a plate with two slices.

"I don't care," said James, covering a warm slice with butter. "Mama-Grace bakes the best bread in the county. That's why she wins prizes at the Fair."

"Well, the best prize is my family's enjoyment of it, warm or cold," Grace smiled at her men, thinking once again how much James had grown.

Jonathan cleared his throat. "How is school going, Son?" he asked.

"Now that we're into English history and literature, it's really got my interest," the boy said. "Father, you were right. The period leading up to the Reformation is exciting. Of course, it's bloody, with heads rolling in every chapter, but it's great to learn about the faith, and the courage of men like Luther and Calvin, and Melanchthon. And today we were reading about the Tudors and the Stuarts. I like the part about John Knox's ministry in Scotland, and the way he tangled with the Queen."

"Tangled' may not be the correct word, Son. Knox was a strongly religious man, and cared deeply for Scotland. He wanted everyone, from Queen Mary on down, to know the freedom they had in Christ, and that they didn't need the Papacy to rule their lives or forgive their sins."

"And he very nearly lost his head because of that."

A smile crept over Jonathan's face. "Yes, he was quoted as saying, 'Presbytery agreeth with the monarchy as God with the devil.'"

James laughed. "He was one fiery preacher. I want to go to

Scotland some day and see where he lived, go to Holyrood Palace, and Edinburgh Cathedral. I bet it still rings with his sermons."

"Perhaps you will, son. Perhaps you will. But first, you need to think about where you'll go to college."

"Oh, Father, I've already decided. Simon and I talk a lot about that. His cousins both went to Davidson, and that's where I really want to go. Mr. Snell says I can complete all my high school course work by next spring, and then he will help me get into college."

"Davidson is a fine school, owned by our denomination." Jonathan commented, processing all his son had said. "I'll see what can be done. You know, we don't have a lot of money."

"Mr. Belk says I can work at his store as long as I like. That would help pay my way through college."

Jonathan smiled. "It seems you have it all figured out. Let me think about this, and talk with your mother."

Grace got up and began removing bowls from the table. "Anyone ready for apple pie?" she asked.

She brought the spicy pastry to the table, along with small plates and forks. After she sliced and served the pie, and then poured coffee for herself and her husband, she looked at James. "Perhaps now is the time to talk with your father about . . ."

"Oh, yes." James jumped in, forking up a bite of the pie. "Father, I've been thinking we should have a Christmas tree this year."

"And what made you think about that? We always celebrate Christmas, and we've never had a tree."

"I know, Father, but Simon . . ."

"Oh, and what has Simon told you?"

"He and his father are going to cut one, out at his grandpa's farm, like they do every year. He invited me to come along and get one for us too."

"You know trees are a pagan tradition."

"Originally they were, I know, but Martin Luther said that Christians could implement that tradition, enjoying God's beautiful creation of the pine tree. And the candles make it a way to proclaim that Jesus is the Light of the world."

"Again, you have all the answers." Jonathan looked across the table at his wife. "Have you been filling his mind with these ideas, Grace?" There was a slight edge to his voice.

"No, Mr. Woolridge. Of course not. He did ask me about a tree, and I told him he'd have to talk with you." She cocked her head. "Mr. Woolridge, I really don't know why you are so dead-set against a Christmas tree. It is a beautiful, festive part of Christmas."

"That's just it. It's festive and . . . and . . . frivolous and takes away from the true meaning of the season."

"Oh no, Father, Christmas is a joyous season because of Jesus' birth, and a tree is just a way to declare all that joy."

Jonathan looked at his son. *When had he begun to think things out for himself?* Clearing his throat again, he said, "The next thing you'll want to do is decorate the tree, and we don't have any . . ."

"Yes we do," Grace broke in.

"What did you say?"

"When Mama died, Mary and I divided up her things, and I have several beautiful tree ornaments and some of the decorations she and I made all those years ago." A slight flush brightened her cheeks.

Jonathan looked at the two of them, took a sip of his coffee, and rose. "I need to do some reading in my study. I'll finish my coffee in there."

After he left, James looked at Grace. "I'm afraid we didn't convince him."

She reached over and patted his hand. "Just you wait, James. I believe your father is thinking about how much we've all missed through the years. I expect he'll come around." She nodded and began clearing the table, so that James could spread out his books and study.

Chapter 19

PASTORING WOES

Grace walked to the living room window and searched the street again. A late September thunderstorm was brewing. She could see the skies darken and hear the wind howling through the ancient oak trees that guarded the front of the house.

"Where are they?" she wondered for the tenth time. "James should have been home from school by now, and Mr. Woolridge was only going to visit a few people at the hospital. What could have happened? That man is nearly sixty, and he pushes himself too much."

Staring into the growing darkness, Grace couldn't help but remember her mother-in-law's gloomy predictions, as she repeatedly described Jonathan's father's death. "He came in from the plant, sat down and died, right there at the kitchen table. Doctor said it was his heart, and him barely sixty-two years old." She always continued, wiping a tear from her eye, "Mark my words, as hard as Jonathan works, it could happen to him, too." Her remarks always left Grace feeling responsible for whatever might happen to her husband.

As she turned, sighed, and made her way to the kitchen, she heard the buggy, and hurried to the back door, a prayer of thanks in her heart.

"Hello, Mama-Grace," called James. "Looks like we barely

made it before the rain." He set the brake, jumped out and ran around to help his father down, then led the team into the barn.

Grace opened the door wide, relief spread across her features. "What caused you to be so late, Mr. Woolridge?"

Jonathan slumped into a kitchen chair. "Mrs. Sommers left word at the hospital for me to come and see her." He nodded at James, who was coming into the room. "I stopped by James' school. It was on the way, and I was glad to have a driver."

"That busy-body!" Exasperation filled Grace's voice. "She just wants to spread gossip, and you are her best source, next to the party line." She went to the stove and poured him a cup of coffee. James came and sat down.

The pastor sighed as he took the cup. "This time she claimed her rheumatism was acting up and she wanted to know if I would pray with her."

"And then did she by any chance mention the rumors about Rachel Honeycutt's daughter, over in Charlotte, living in a boarding house with both men and women?"

He took a sip of his coffee. "Yes, she hinted that I should know about that, but I guess I was too tired after making the hospital visits, to show the expected interest. I told her I didn't see that was anyone else's business." He smiled at her over the rim of the cup. "I don't think she liked my answer."

Grace sat down at the table just as James started laughing. "Father, tell her about Mrs. Sommers chasing us down the lane with her broom."

"No, she didn't!" Grace couldn't keep the laughter out of her voice.

"Now, James. It was just that her steps needed sweeping, and we were going anyway."

By that time Grace was laughing so hard she had to wipe her eyes with a napkin.

Jonathan, trying to hide a smile, said, "Son, I don't want to hear any more of that kind of disrespect from your lips. That lady is a member of our congregation and deserves our attention just as the others do."

"But she seems to need more than the rest of the congregation put together," Grace said. "For the life of me, Mr. Woolridge, I don't know why you can't see that."

Jonathon put his cup down. "Grace, you know I'm called to serve all these people." A smile teased his lips. "I really have no choice."

Grace rose and went to the window. "I'm just grateful you're both home safely. This looks like a real storm, and that buggy is flimsy protection." She turned. "Will you two be ready for supper in an hour? I've been putting together a pot of soup, with the vegetables Mrs. Brown dropped off this morning."

Jonathan refilled his coffee cup and headed toward the stairs. "That's fine. I have some reading I need to do," he said.

James went to the refrigerator and took out the milk pitcher, then got a glass from the cabinet. "Got any of that good pound cake left, Mama-Grace?" he asked.

"Not this close to supper, James."

The boy sighed and gulped down his milk.

Chapter 20

A NEW SEASON

Brisk winds whipped the branches of a maple outside the parlor window. Grace sat at the small desk writing a letter.
March 17, 1922
My Dear Sister,
I still find it hard to believe that we have moved once again, and to Mississippi! After twenty years of ministry in North Carolina, Mr. Woolridge has taken a pastorate in Jackson, Mississippi, of all places. I have never questioned his decisions until this one. He explained that, at his age, it was a great opportunity, becoming an assistant pastor in a city church. I knew his duties at Pegram Street Church, and as Stated Clerk of Mecklenburg Presbytery, as well as General Assembly's Mission Board kept him much too busy. Yet, it was almost like the old days, Mary. He kept me up many nights, sharing stories and concerns, even asking my advice at times. I think he was beginning to crave a change, though, when the call came from this church. The elders say they need a Visitation Pastor. He's certainly good at that, but I don't know how much preaching he'll do with two other pastors on staff.
And James is about to graduate from college. We both long to be there, but how can we possibly make that long trip again, in less than three months?

James has grown into a gracious and reliable young man, looking forward to seminary. When he was home for Christmas, he couldn't stop talking about his dreams of traveling in Scotland, and of becoming a pastor. Working for Mr. Belk, at his dry goods store in Charlotte has been good experience for him, and he delights in meeting all kinds of people there. Of course his father is very proud, but I do miss him so. He was the light and laughter of this family. I keep listening for his footsteps, the clatter of the screen door, and the sound of his voice. He always had stories to tell us. What an imagination! Of course I, too, am proud of his accomplishments and pray daily for him to do well, but my heart is heavy these days.

You are the only one to whom I can talk about this sadness, and my growing concern for Mr. Woolridge's health. He caught a cold, just days after the move, and his cough is deep and harsh. It keeps him from sleeping, but he won't listen to my pleas to call the doctor.

I know I'm just being a worry-wort. Probably everything is fine, but I can't help but recall Mother Woolridge's stories about Jonathan's father's death at sixty-two.

I was happy to hear of Elizabeth's new baby. You must be a very proud grandmother. What a joy to have them close by, there in Raleigh. It seems no time since we were there for the wedding, but it has been three years already, and our children are grown up.

I'm about to finish the crocheted blanket and will get it in the mail soon. I hope she enjoys snuggling under it. How I wish I could see her and her mama!

Please pray for my spirit, in this alien place. The people seem so different here in the city. They have all been kind and welcoming, but I miss our simple country folk. And the woman who works here at the manse is a great talker, but not much of a worker. I'm still unpacking boxes, after nearly three weeks.

    Your loving sister,
     Grace

Grace folded the letter and addressed the envelope. For a long while, she sat in the big arm chair looking out at the feathery green of the dogwoods, this early spring day. Her thoughts drifted back to the huge homestead at Stem. She and her siblings lived such happy lives, cared for by wealthy, protective parents. She smiled as she remembered riding with Jonathan those spring afternoons when they were falling in love. She felt a tear creep down her cheek as she thought of the delightful, challenging little boy James had been, how he welcomed her love, and the joy they found as a family. Then, the hopes that were dashed when she lost her baby. That sad time seemed to change everything, though they continued daily life, Jonathan working hard as a pastor, she laboring to make a safe, happy home for the three of them. But she missed those times when they could show love for each other, when she thought he was healing from the loss of Kate. They even laughed together then, as he read to her many nights, once James was in bed. That was before the miscarriage, before Jonathan retreated into his private sadness. Had she done enough to try and bring him back from that solitary place? To bridge that gap for James? Had she made the home warm and loving enough to make up for his father's indifference? And his grandmother's constant whining and criticism?

She bowed her head. *Father, I'm so ashamed. You have been my loving Friend and Guide through all these years, and You've given me a good husband and a son to love. Now, Father, make me content with whatever you have for our future. And, please, take care of Mr. Woolridge. I love him so. All he's ever wanted to do was to serve You. And now, his son is preparing for the Gospel ministry. What a blessing.* She sighed and stood as she heard the carriage's wheels in the lane. It would soon be time for supper.

She heard footsteps, the door opening, then a strange moan. Heart pounding, she raced to the kitchen.

Chapter 21

END OF A MINISTRY
MARCH 18, 1922

Before her eyes her husband slumped to the kitchen floor. Terrified, Grace knelt and took his limp hand in hers. "Mr. Woolridge!" she cried. "Mr. Woolridge, speak to me."

No response. Pressing her fingers to his throat, she found a faint pulse, and leaned close to hear his raspy breathing.

I must call someone. Who? Rising on shaky legs, she went to the telephone. Reading from a list on the nearby counter, she took down the receiver and asked the operator to ring Dr. McDonald, an officer in their church whom Grace had met once.

Though it seemed much longer, it was only minutes before the doctor arrived. Grace led him to the kitchen where he knelt to examine Jonathan. Slowly he stood. "Mrs. Woolridge, your husband appears to have an advanced case of pneumonia. I'll get someone over here to move him to his bed, but I'm afraid all we can do is try and make him comfortable. I'll send for some medicine, and we'll watch him closely, but . . ." His voice trailed off, as he began packing his bag.

Grace wanted to scream, but only nodded. She discovered she was sobbing. The doctor led her to a chair, and then began barking orders into the telephone. Grace couldn't take her eyes off the man she had loved for nearly twenty years. Soon three gentlemen from the church arrived, gently lifted the pastor and took him to their bedroom down the hall.

The back door opened and Grace saw the worried face of a woman she had met at the church's welcoming reception, just two weeks earlier. She laid a tender hand on Grace's shoulder and said, "Mrs. Woolridge, I'm Sadie McDonald, the doctor's wife. I'm so sorry about your husband, but I will stay with you as long as you need me." She sat at the table beside Grace. "Is there someone I can call? Your son, a relative?"

Grace looked up at the kind face. "James," she said. "Yes, James must be told. But he's so far away, in North Carolina."

"Don't you worry about that. Just give me an address and telephone number. One of the men will go and get him for you."

A few minutes later, she made a call. "Hiram," she said, "Pastor Woolridge has been taken seriously ill with pneumonia. We don't know any more. The doctor is with him. We need someone to go to Davidson College in North Carolina and bring his son home." She smiled and then said, "Thank you, Hiram. I thought you would. Here's the address." She read from Grace's address book. "Just call this number at the school. Tell them his father is very ill and needs him to come home."

The afternoon passed in a blur. Someone from the drug store delivered supplies to the doctor, and he forced a spoonful of liquid past the parched lips of his patient, who slept deeply, an ominous rattling sound in his chest. Grace found a chair beside the bed where she took up a vigil, holding the limp hand and speaking softly to her husband.

Lights were turned on in the living room and kitchen, women organized a meal, answered the telephone, and greeted visitors. Kind voices urged Grace to eat. They brought her coffee and a cup of soup, both left untouched. Sometime during the night her head drooped on the bed, and someone put a blanket around her shoulders. She woke with a start, as soft rays of dawn light shone through the window. Grace leaned over to touch her husband's cheek. He was still breathing.

Sadie came and laid a warm hand on Grace's shoulder. "Mrs. Woolridge, we've sent for your son. Hiram is on his way to North Carolina, he left around six last night. He hopes to bring young James home before suppertime."

She slipped a hand under Grace's elbow. "You really must come downstairs and get some breakfast, Mrs. Woolridge. I have coffee on and oatmeal cooking. The ladies from church have brought in several casseroles."

Grace nodded. "I know." She tried to smile as she rose to her feet. Glancing at the beloved face once more, she turned to follow her new friend. She tried to eat, but the food was tasteless, and she felt anxious to get back to the bedroom. *What if he should rally, and not see her there?*

Toward noon, Grace let the ladies persuade her to rest for an hour and change clothes. Dr. McDonald was with Jonathan. Later, Grace realized that she needed to call Mary and Samuel. However, when she heard her sister's voice, her own failed her, and she fell to weeping. Sadie took over.

"Mrs. White? This is Sadie McDonald, a member of First Presbyterian Church in Jackson. I am afraid I have some rather sad news. Pastor Woolridge has a very serious case of pneumonia. He is unresponsive . . . Yes, one of the men has gone to Davidson, to bring his son home. Of course, we'll take good care of Mrs. Woolridge. We'll let you know any further developments."

As the day darkened, one of the ladies brought a tray and coaxed Grace to eat a few bites of stew. The lamp on the dresser was turned on while Grace kept vigil, hoping every minute to hear the familiar voice.

It was close to midnight when James entered the bedroom, his reddened eyes filled with questions and pain. Grace took him in her arms, and after a moment he leaned over the man on the bed and said, "Father, it's James. Please speak to me."

Grace was sure she saw a faint movement of Jonathan's

eyelids, then nothing.

Grace wiped her tears at this scene of fresh pain. Then she began to answer the questions in her son's eyes.

"I heard a strange sound just as he came into the kitchen, from an afternoon call," she said, looking into the beloved brown eyes. "I . . . I found him there, lying on the floor. He was so still, and I tried to talk to him, but he never heard me." She stopped to blow her nose and wipe the flowing tears. "His pulse was very weak, and I didn't know what to do, so I sent for the doctor. He says your father has a serious case of pneumonia."

She settled back in her chair and sighed. "I've been worried about him. He's been so tired, and caught a cold right after the move. The cough has gotten worse, keeping him up at night, but he wouldn't see the doctor." She shook her head and caressed her husband's hand. It was so cold!

The doctor slipped in, put a strong hand on James' shoulder, and said, "Son, I'm so sorry." He took out his stethoscope. A moment later, he lifted the sheet and covered the pastor's face.

"I'm sorry, Mrs. Woolridge. He's gone from us."

She knew she should hold up and be brave, but she laid her head on her husband's quiet chest and wept great heaving sobs. After a moment, she felt James' arms around her.

"Mama-Grace," he choked out, "Why did he have to leave us? I had so much to tell him, so many questions to ask."

She wiped at her tears and patted his arm. "I don't know, James. But I know that God will never leave us, and we must trust Him now, more than we ever have."

Sadie McDonald came into the room. "You two need to come downstairs and eat something. We've called the funeral home and Mr. Hendricks will be here shortly. He'll want to speak with you."

In the days that followed, Grace walked in a daze of grief, making decisions with James at her side. After a short service at the church, Jonathan's body was sent by train to a funeral home in Oxford for burial.

By telephone, Mary and Samuel welcomed her into their home, until she could make a decision about where to live. Kind people from the church packed up the family's belongings, and within the week, Grace and James were on a train for North Carolina, accompanied by the church's senior pastor. The day after their arrival, she stood at the family plot Jonathan had bought for Kate in Oxford's Elmwood cemetery and said her final goodbyes to the man she loved, whose life was her calling, her fulfillment and joy.

The morning was gray, with rain spattering the windows. Grace sat, still in her dressing gown, in the guest room of her sister's home in Raleigh. At the sound of a light knock on the door, she looked up to welcome her son.

"Mama-Grace," he said, coming to sit on the bed beside her and taking her hand. "It's time for me to go back to school."

She studied his beloved face. "I know, James," she said.

"I hate to leave you, but I've lost two weeks, and graduation is coming soon."

His arms went around her, and she wept against his shoulder.

Then she raised her eyes to his and said, "You have a legacy to carry on, and graduating from college is the beginning of that. Don't worry about me. I'm cared for here, and perhaps we can travel to Davidson for your graduation." She worked hard at a brave smile. "Did you see what they'll be inscribing on your father's gravestone?"

He nodded. "Minister of the Gospel of Jesus Christ in the Presbyterian Church." He smiled. "That's exactly what he was."

James rose to go. "Uncle Samuel is taking me to the bus. I'll call you tonight." He stooped to kiss her cheek, and left.

For a long time, Grace stared at the rain sliding down the window. In the space of a few days, her life had taken a wrenching turn. She had lost her identity as spouse, pastor's wife, even mother. She was a different person, and oh, how she wished she knew who that person was.

Church started by John E. Wool
(one of five in Southwestern Virginia)

Mr. and Mrs. Henry Preston
request the honor of your presence
at the marriage of their sister,
Katharine Kelly
to
Rev. John Ellis Wool,
Wednesday afternoon, June twenty-seventh,
nineteen hundred,
at half past two o'clock.
Presbyterian Church.
Tazewell, Virginia.

Wedding invitation of Katharine Kelly
and John Ellis Wool, June 27, 1900

Portrait of Katharine Rachella Kelly, 1900

*John Ellis Wool, circa 1900,
in Alpaca suit and celluloid collar*

*Katharine Rachella Kelly's
wedding portrait, June 1900*

Grandmother Wool (Elmira Demarest Wool)
with James Craig Wool II, in baptismal dress,
August 1901

Grandmother Wool with James Craig Wool II,
(about 3 years old)

John Ellis Wool
shortly before his death in 1922

Chapter 22

RELUCTANT CHANGE

Grace wondered if she'd ever get used to the noise of a busy city. It was late summer in Raleigh, and uncomfortably hot. She gazed out the window of her upstairs room at the kitchen garden which still blessed the family with fresh vegetables. The roses were vibrant around the side porch, and huge, old mimosa trees filled the yard with color.

She started at the sound of her sister's voice, asking, "May I come in?"

"Oh, Mary. I must have been day-dreaming again." She turned and tried to smile.

"I'm sorry to disturb you, Grace, but Elizabeth just phoned, and is bringing little Anna by for a visit." She walked over and sat on the bed. "I'm sure you'll want to come down and join us."

Absently, Grace put a hand to her hair. "Yes, I . . . I'll just need a few minutes."

Mary rose and turned toward the door. "That's fine, dear. Just come down when you're ready. We missed you at breakfast. Would you like a cup of coffee?"

"No. No thank you." Grace turned toward her dressing table. "I'll be down shortly."

Grace looked at the sad image of herself in the mirror. The

disheveled hair, dark circles under her eyes filled with deep sadness, the droop of her mouth. *How long can this go on?* She thought, picking up a brush. *I don't seem to have any 'gumption' at all. It's been four months, and I still can't think clearly.* Familiar tears formed in her eyes, and she wiped them away with a lacy handkerchief. *What a burden I am to my dear sister and her family. Perhaps I need to consider Joe's offer to move to Oxford, and help out at the church there. Am I ready for something new?*

She brushed her gray locks into a tight bun and pinned it up. *Oh, Mr. Woolridge, what have you done to me. . .to all of us?* She sighed as she picked up a powder puff and patted her face.

James walked slowly down the steps from the store's small office, where he had given his letter of resignation to Mr. Belk's secretary. In a week he would be traveling to Richmond, Virginia, where he had been accepted as a student at Union Theological Seminary. After paying the money for his tuition, room and board for one semester, there was barely enough left for train fare.

O Lord, he prayed as he walked to his boarding house, *please give me a church that will let me come and preach, so I can pay the rest of the year's expens*es. The seminary office had assured him that most of their students took weekend preaching assignments, and his name was being considered. He thought of his father, of long rides in the buggy discussing his sermon. *Am I doing this for Father?* he wondered, *or is it truly the desire of my heart?*

Reaching his room, he sat on the narrow bed and put his head in his hands. If only he could share this moment of uncertainty with the man he admired most in life. He remembered the shock of his father's death, just weeks before they were to celebrate his graduation from Davidson. Now, he was off to seminary, and the pain of missing that great man went deep into his soul.

Chapter 23

NEW SCHOOL, NEW LIFE

Huge, ancient trees graced the Richmond, Virginia campus where stately brick buildings spoke of history and purpose. As James approached the grounds after his walk from the train station, he stopped, set down his bag and stared. This was the place where he would receive the training he needed to be a minister of the Gospel. His heart swelled with joy even as his mind filled with apprehension and questions.

The first question was soon answered. A student who seemed to know his way around walked up to him and asked, "Are you looking for the registrar's office?"

James laughed with relief. "Yes," he said, "how did you know?"

The young man nodded toward James' worn suitcase and grinned. "Come on. It's this way." He stuck out his hand. "I'm John Williams," he said. "I'm a Middler, and we're supposed to be on the lookout for lost freshmen."

"Well, that's me. My name's James, and I'm about as lost as they come."

"Oh, you'll feel at home in no time. We're a pretty small, close-knit student body. Where'd you go to college?"

"Davidson, down in North Carolina."

"Yeah, I know Davidson, got a brother going there this fall.

I finished at UNC. My folks live in Raleigh."

A small pain somewhere around his heart startled James.

As they were about to enter a building with a plaque which read, *Administration,* another student approached, also carrying a suitcase.

"Another lost freshman," said John, and waved. The three entered together.

James breathed in the scent of old wood and musty books. The air of the place felt both ancient and excitingly new.

At the second door John stopped, swung it open and ushered the two young men inside. They were greeted by a short man with thin white hair and a huge smile. "Welcome to Union Theological Seminary," the Dean said.

Later, as James unpacked his few belongings, he felt a pang of homesickness. When he went to Davidson, it was only a short drive back home, and he returned often during those years, until his folks moved to Mississippi.

Where was home now? Father was gone and Mama-Grace lived with Cousin Joe in Oxford. He'd never be able to stride into her kitchen and enjoy the welcoming aroma of fresh-baked bread, along with those loving arms, always opened wide to greet him.

James stepped to the window. A breeze stirred the branches of an oak tree just outside. He looked out at the campus where he would be working and studying the next three years. He thought of his fathe*r,* and a familiar heaviness came over him. How he longed to share this day, this beginning, with the one who had walked this very campus so many years before.

Footsteps in the hall announced his roommate. James turned around to greet a young man a few inches taller than himself, with sunburned hair and a ruddy complexion.

"I'm Rob," he said, slinging two bags onto one of the narrow beds.

James thrust out his hand, "James."

"Can I call you 'Jim'?"

For a moment, James hesitated. He'd never been called

anything but James. Then he grinned. "Sounds good to me." Just one more thing for him to get used to in this new life called Seminary.

As they unpacked, deciding each one's space, Rob asked, "Where you from, Jim?"

"Last place I lived was Cornelius, down in North Carolina, but . . ." James swallowed a troublesome lump in his throat.

Rob opened the small closet and hung up three jackets with matching slacks. "Folks still there?" he asked casually.

"My father . . . was . . . a pastor there, until he moved to Mississippi, where he died." James' voice trailed off as he busied himself arranging underwear in a drawer.

Rob moved closer, his eyes full of puzzled pain. "Ah, Jim, I'm sorry. I didn't mean to pry."

James forced a smile, "It's okay, Rob. That's just how it is. My stepmother is with some of her family in Oxford, North Carolina, so I guess that's where I'll be spending my holiday time. I lived there once, but don't remember much about the town." He began arranging books on his desk.

Rob asked, "Is there anyone else? A brother or sister?"

"No, it's just been the three of us for as long as I can remember." He looked up at his new friend. "What about your family? Do they live in Virginia?"

"Yeah, my dad's business is in Roanoke." He grinned. "He wasn't too happy about my decision to come here."

Relieved that the conversation had shifted, James asked, "Why? Doesn't he like preachers?"

"Not much. He's a member of the church. He's even an elder, but I guess his dream was for me to take over the family business, and I just couldn't do that."

"What made you decide on seminary?"

"My pastor, actually. He helped me through some tough times as a rebellious teenager, and I wanted what he had. He taught me more about God's grace, and His claims on my life than I'd ever learned in eighteen years of attending Sunday School."

"It must have been hard, telling your dad."

"Hardest thing I ever did. My mom was happy about my decision, but my dad . . ."

"Did he 'disinherit' you?" James asked with a grin.

"No, my mom wouldn't stand for that, but I knew he was really disappointed with my choice." Rob sat on his bunk. "He never wanted my brother around the business, but it looks like he's the one who will take it over, after all, when he finishes college next year."

A knock on the open door interrupted their conversation. "Hey, you freshmen. Time to get over to Old Main for orientation." A short, wiry fellow with dark, tousled curls and snapping black eyes came bouncing into the room. "I'm Jason Wilkes, your Senior Adviser. I'm down at the end of the hall, if you need anything." He turned and was gone.

"Hope we don't need anything." Rob laughed. "He seems pretty important."

"Yeah," James remarked. "He thinks so."

As the two young men walked across campus, James had an eerie feeling of his father's presence, in the rustle of the trees overhead, and the aroma of antiquity as they entered the main campus building.

Chapter 24

BORROWED MEMORIES

Cloudy skies produced misting rain as Jim and Rob followed the crowd of students and sightseers down the historic mile from Holyrood Palace to the ancient stone walls of St. Giles Cathedral in Edinburgh, Scotland. Though it was the middle of a weekday as they entered the basilica, the melodic strains of a Bach choral echoed in the stillness. The two seminary students stood open-mouthed for several minutes, listening, taking in the sight of ancient stone walls blackened by the flames of a million candles, enriched by worship of saints and sinners gathered to hear sermons delivered from the high, walled pulpit in the center of the cross-shaped church. Small side chapels held low benches, and a few worshipers could be seen bowed in prayer. Tall, stained glass windows gave softened light, as the music paused and then pealed forth a deafening anthem.

"Do you feel it?" Rob asked in a hushed tone.

"What?"

"The spirits of the Scottish Covenanters, worshiping here at the risk of their lives, refusing to kneel, as the Church of England required." He grinned. "Stubborn lot, our Reformed forefathers."

Jim nodded, "I can hear John Knox thundering from that high

pulpit, about salvation by grace alone. "

"And the tramp of boots as Queen Mary's guards stormed the place."

"And Knox shouting, 'Presbytery agreeth with the monarchy as God with the devil!' They're all here, and this church seems to be thriving on the Gospel, even after four centuries."

The two young men slipped into a side chapel and instinctively bowed their heads as they seated themselves on a bare bench.

They were no longer tourists as they had been, traveling through Germany, England, and now Scotland. They were part of the Church Militant, worshiping a Timeless God, marching with saints gone before them.

Later, they enjoyed fish and chips at a pub down the street. "Tomorrow we board that freighter for the trip home," Rob said, lifting a very-American Coca-Cola bottle to his lips.

Jim grinned. "That doesn't sound nearly as exciting as it did a month ago."

"Right, but it will get us home, and I'm ready," Rob responded. "What will you remember about our trip?"

Jim chewed a moment, before he responded. "I'll never forget the thrill of standing at the door to the Wittenburg Chapel, knowing I was on the very spot where the Protestant Reformation began. I was blindsided by the courage of Martin Luther to post those ninety-five theses, fully aware he was taking on the mighty Roman Church. What a man!" He shook his head in wonder and a bit of awe.

"But don't forget the ink spot on the wall of his house," Rob interjected. "He was hounded by all the insecurities that plague you and me. Old Satan was real enough to him, apparently."

"So real that he threw the ink bottle at him." They both laughed.

"The castles and cathedrals are amazing, though. Imagine how many thousands of man-hours it took to build them. Makes you wonder if any of the people who worked on those walls ever got to live or worship there."

Rob finished his Coke. "Probably not. They were serfs, virtual slaves building for the glory of their kings."

Jim crunched on his last chip. "The saddest part is that so many of those beautiful cathedrals aren't even churches any more. Did you notice how many, even here in Edinburgh, are museums, or libraries, or even pubs?

"Says something really sad about the state of faith here and on the continent, after all the preaching, and bloodshed of the martyrs."

Jim grinned, "Those are gloomy thoughts for a couple of fellows on a school holiday."

They rose, paid their bills, and walked out into thin sunshine.

Passing St. Giles on the way to their student hostel, Jim remarked, "You know, I believe the highlight of this whole trip was the time we spent right there, in that church. I . . . felt a sense of fellowship not only with Knox, the martyrs and others who have worshiped there, but . . . with God Himself. I think I felt something like a renewed, or confirmed call to Gospel ministry." He looked at his friend. "Does that sound far-fetched to you?"

"Not far-fetched, but a bit frightening."

"How so?"

"We've just been in the presence of history, and history is made up of fighting and bloodshed. Especially for those called by God, like John Knox, Luther, Melancthon, the Scottish Covenanters, all the Reformers."

After a long moment, Jim said, "Uh, I hear what you're saying. Answering a call to Gospel ministry could be dangerous. I remember times when my father dared to speak out against wrongs he saw in our community. We were asked to leave one pastorate, and Father went through some serious bouts of depression."

"Better be sure you know what you're doing."

Jim hesitated at the steps of the building where they were staying. "Rob, I honestly don't think I have any choice."

"We are both called by a Mighty God to preach His Gospel

of Judgment, Forgiveness and Grace," Rob added, nodding.

"Right, to people who desperately need grace, like us, and don't know it yet," Jim mused, "and who may not want to hear this Gospel of freedom from sin and new life in Christ."

His friend laid an arm about his shoulders. "I know what you mean, Jim, and I do believe we've been forewarned." They entered their room, as Rob added, softly, "There was a reason this was the final stop on our whirlwind tour of Europe."

Chapter 25

SO SWEET IN THE SPRINGTIME

Grace settled into her favorite rocker and smiled at her sister, who was visiting from Raleigh. She had a comfortable suite in her brother Joe's home in Oxford.

"Grace, I'm afraid you're working too hard. We aren't young any more, you know," Mary said, as she picked up her teacup and took a sip.

"Sometimes I agree with you," Grace sighed, "but it's good to feel useful again. The church needed a hostess for the Wednesday night dinners, and I do enjoy the pastoral visiting. This young pastor is getting acquainted with his flock, and I already know many of these families."

Her sister laughed. "You should. We're kin to most of them." She picked up a ginger cookie.

"The church has been a lifesaver for me," Grace said. "You remember how miserable I was in the months after Jonathan's death, the move, and then James leaving for Seminary. I didn't know who I was or what I was supposed to do."

Mary nodded. "I remember. I was so sorry for you, but I didn't know how to help." She took another sip, and asked, "What do you hear from James these days?"

"He's working hard and making good grades, all the while filling the pulpit at the Blacksburg church." Grace stirred her tea. "You know he and his roommate went to Europe last summer—on a freighter."

Mary laughed. "I heard about that. It sounded wonderful to me!"

"But on a freighter? And they were backpacking and staying in student hostels. Anything could have happened."

Mary put a hand on Grace's arm. "Mama-Grace, you worry too much about your sweet boy. He's grown up now, and capable of making his own decisions."

"I know, and God took good care of those boys, 'way over there in those foreign countries. You know, James has talked about going to Scotland since he was in high school." She sighed. "I just wish he'd find a wonderful girl up there in Richmond. He'll be out of school and ready to take a church in another year."

"Something else God can manage. I'm sure He has great plans for our young man. Samuel is looking around for a spot in our Presbytery. It would be so good to have him close by."

Grace picked up a cookie. "Everyone needs a place to belong, where they're needed. James will find his place, I'm sure. He says he truly enjoys preaching in the Blacksburg church, though it keeps him busy, and I rarely ever see him."

She got up and refilled their teacups. "All those years, I was content to be at Jonathan's side in the pastorate, and raising James. Right now, my place is here, serving again in our first pastorate."

"Remember what I said earlier, about coming to Raleigh for a visit, Dear. Samuel and I are rattling around in that big house, and need company. Of course, Elizabeth brings the baby around almost every day, and Sarah is home from Queens some weekends. but we still have oodles of room."

"I promise I'll visit soon. We won't have church suppers in the summer, but I'm not sure about James' schedule. I'll let you know more, closer to the time. I can hardly wait to hold that sweet baby again, and visit with both your girls. It's been so long since I've had time with them."

Mary glanced out the window. "There's Samuel, ready to go home after his long meeting, I'm sure." She smiled as she picked up her pocketbook and looped its strap over her arm. She leaned over to kiss her sister's cheek. "We'll be waiting to hear about your visit," she said, as they both walked to the door and greeted Samuel.

As Jim crossed the familiar campus to deliver a paper to his Homiletics professor, he noticed that the air seemed softer. Breezes stirred the ancient cedars, and the maples and dogwoods were suddenly full of tiny green leaves. It was the spring of his Middle year.

"Wait up, Jim," he heard Rob's voice. He turned and noticed two young women walking with his friend. He recognized Carrie; a girl Rob had dated several times.

"Want you to meet someone." As they approached, he said, "Jim, this is Carolyn O'Bryant. She and Carrie are roommates over at the Training School. We need another fellow for a picnic this Saturday."

She was nearly as tall as he, with golden-brown curls dancing wildly around a creamy complexion, and emerald-green eyes that instantly mesmerized him. *She must be Irish*, he thought.

"What do you say, Jim? Got time for a picnic?"

"Y . . . es, I think so," he stammered.

"Great." Rob turned to Carrie. "We'll pick you girls up at your dorm at noon. Jim's preaching Sunday, so we can't keep him out late." He laughed and slapped his friend on the back. Jim never felt it. He stood and stared as the two girls headed off toward their own campus across the street.

Chapter 26

ROMANCE AT MASSANETTA

The shouts and laughter of a hundred campers began to die away, as the sun set on another day at the Massanetta Springs Conference Center nestled in the Shenandoah Valley of Virginia.

Jim whistled softly as he walked along a trail that led to the center of the conference grounds. Inside her cabin, Carolyn heard, "When Irish Eyes Are Smiling" and slipped quietly out the screen door to meet the man who made her heart sing, and her own Irish eyes smile.

They met at the flag pole and found a seat on a low stone wall. They had been dating, mostly in the company of other Seminary and Training School couples, off and on for nearly two years. As she smoothed her skirt and sat down, Carolyn wondered if Jim could hear the pounding of her heart, at his nearness.

Jim's smile lighted the darkness. He took her hand as soon as they were seated. "I have some great news," he said. "Today I received a letter from the church I told you about, at Stuart's Draft."

She caught her breath. "I remember. You preached there a couple of times in June."

"They've just built a new building, and want a pastor to help them grow. It's an old congregation, mostly farmers, but the most genuine people I've ever met. I felt a real call, even before I got the letter."

She couldn't help but share his excitement. But she had news of her own. "Oh, Jim, I'm so glad. When do you meet with the Pulpit Committee?"

"They want me to preach this Sunday, and meet with the Committee in the afternoon."

"I just know they're going to call you!"

He laughed, "That would be good. The church in Blacksburg has called a full-time pastor, and I'm out of a job at the end of August." He added, "and then there's the ordination examination by Presbytery next week." He let go of her hand and stood. "That one scares me a little." He turned to face her. "It actually scares me a whole lot!"

"Why?" she asked, her brow wrinkling a bit.

"I sat in on Rob's examination last spring, and those men are seasoned pastors who know their theology. The questions are pretty thorough. Bible knowledge, church history, theology, homiletics, hermeneutics, reasons for entering the ministry." He sighed. "The Presbytery fathers are really concerned about that, and understandably so."

She stood and they began walking toward the mess hall. "Oh, Jim, you're going to do fine on that examination. You've just finished three years of studying everything they could ask you, and look at your grades." She took his hand. "After all, you're in God's hands, and He's ready to use you mightily in His church."

"I really hope so. I can see myself serving that congregation. The church is small, but they have a really nice manse just up the hill. I've already written Mama-Grace about coming to keep house for me, for a while." He looked down at her.

Was he thinking she might eventually live in that manse? Her heart fluttered at the invitation in his eyes. She knew she loved him. Did he feel the same?

She studied the path they were walking, and said, "I'll pray for you, and for the church." She turned to him. "I have some news too." At the question on his face, she went on. "You know how much I've loved working at Second Presbyterian in Richmond, since I finished the Training School. There have been some staff changes, and I was afraid they wouldn't need me anymore." She smiled at the look of concern on his face. "Well," she said, wonder in her voice, "today I got a telephone call from the pastor, asking me to be his personal secretary, with a raise in salary!"

"Hooray for Christmas!" Jim said, pulling her into an exuberant hug. "Will your mother stay on with you?"

"I don't know." she answered, a bit flustered at being in his arms. She laughed lightly. "I'm not sure Cammie and I can get along without her wonderful meals. She's lived with us ever since we graduated from the Training School, last year."

They turned to walk back to her cabin area, holding hands. "Looks like God is calling both of us into new ministry this summer," Jim said.

She turned to him, seeing what she was sure was love, in those deep brown eyes. "I . . . I need to go, before one of my girls has a bad dream, and wakes the others. I'd never get them settled down again."

"Yeah, my boys are probably up to some kind of mischief by now, too." He grinned.

They stood, hand-in-hand, for a moment. "Goodnight, Jim," she said, and stood on tiptoe to place a kiss on his cheek. Quickly she turned and fled toward her cabin.

Glancing over her shoulder, she saw Jim standing in the shadows, his hand on the spot where the sweetness of her kiss lingered.

𝔠𝔥𝔞𝔭𝔱𝔢𝔯 27

PROMISES AND A PASTORATE
MARCH 18, 1931

"Something old, something new, something borrowed, something blue, and a lucky sixpence in her shoe," Cammie chanted as she slipped the cream lace gown over Carolyn's head.

The bride laughed nervously. "Yes, Mama's Bible, your handkerchief tucked into my bouquet, my new dress and veil." She arranged the band of silk orange blossoms among her thick curls, to anchor the gauzy veil.

"The blue garter," Cammie reminded her, and laughed at Carolyn's blushing cheeks.

"And here's the lucky sixpence for your shoe," the bride's mother, Annie, announced as she entered the upstairs bedroom of the old manse.

"I thought those boys would never leave last night," sighed Cammie. "For a bunch of young preachers, they were having a high old time."

"Jim is so thoughtful to make arrangements at the boarding house for the three of them, so we ladies could have the manse," Annie said.

Carolyn turned around slowly and gazed about her. "This is the room I'll be coming back to as a bride. This lovely old house will be my home, and I'll be the preacher's wife." She touched the fruit carvings on the head of the bed as wonder filled her eyes with surprise tears.

Her mother touched her cheek. "Bride's nerves, Honey?" she asked.

"Mama, do you remember, when I'd fall and hit my elbow, and you'd say, 'That's the way you feel when you get married.'?"

Annie smiled and nodded, as Carolyn continued, "I think that's how I'm feeling now . . . kind of surprised, a little sad, exhilarated, and even out-of-control. Does that sound silly?"

"It sounds like every bride who ever prepared to see her life changed forever."

"Oh, Mama!" Carolyn bent to hug her diminutive mother, who had to brush away her own tears.

The bride looked at her reflection in the long mirror on the back of the door. "I still can't believe Jim wants me for his wife, and that we'll share this pastorate." *And this bed*, she thought, as a shiver went up her spine.

"God is indeed good to you, my dear," her mother said, straightening up the dresser.

"I wish Jim's 'Mama-Grace' could have lived a few more months, and been here with us. I only met her once, but the church ladies really loved her." Carolyn sighed.

"And so did Jim. She was a good mother to him, all those years," Annie said. Then she turned to her daughter, "But God knows exactly what He's doing, bringing you here to this lovely valley, to be Jim's helpmate, and serve these people."

She walked to the window. "The Auxiliary ladies outdid themselves on your bridal luncheon today. The church basement looks like a garden. I can't imagine where they got all those flowers, here in the middle of March."

"And the food! These folks know how to cook. Maybe you can take some lessons from them, Carolyn," Cammie hinted, as she picked up Carolyn's discarded wool dress from a chair and hung it in the closet.

"They are an interesting group. Remember how I had my heart set on a St. Patrick's Day wedding? But they were hosting the Spring Presbyterial Meeting yesterday, and made sure I knew it. So-o-o-o we're getting married on March 18th. It's been a busy two days for them."

"You'll soon be part of all that," Cammie said, and straightened the veil to frame the bride's face. "Quite a change from running a big city church."

"You're right," Carolyn responded, "but more challenging, since I'll have a husband to take care of, as well."

Annie turned from the window. "Rob is here with the car, to take us to the church." The three ladies picked up warm shawls and headed downstairs.

In the car, Annie admitted to being nervous. "I've never given a bride away," she said. "I didn't know it could be done."

Carolyn hugged her mother. "Well, we're doing it, Mama," she said. "I only wish Augusta were here."

"So do I, but she's too close to having that baby to make the long trip from Milwaukee. I'll be writing her all the details tonight, and I'll send some pictures later."

With sprays of pink and white flowers on the front doors, Finley Memorial Presbyterian church welcomed its pastor's bride. Rob escorted the ladies to a room at the back of the sanctuary, and went to stand beside his friend at the front.

Minutes later the vestibule doors opened, the organ pealed out the Bridal Chorus, and Cammie, as Maid of Honor, began her stately walk down the aisle. The minister with whom Carolyn had worked for the past three years stood at the front with a nervous but broadly grinning groom and his two seminary friends.

Carolyn slipped her hand into the crook of her mother's arm, and they entered the sanctuary as the congregation stood.

To love and to cherish, in sickness and in health, in joy and in sorrow, keeping myself only unto you, so long as we both shall live. They pledged their love and faith, each to the other. The minister pronounced them man and wife, before the members of Jim's congregation.

"What therefore God hath joined together, let not man put asunder," he warned, and blessed the couple bowed before him.

The organist began the triumphant recessional. Jim kissed his bride, and they walked up the aisle, into a life of service together.

Chapter 28

A NEW CRY, A NEW CALL
1933

Carolyn walked heavily, to answer the knock on the manse's front door. She was feeling very pregnant, this dreary February day, and wished Jim were home from visiting the Varner family, over in the village of Stuart's Draft.

Outside, snow swirled past the windows, promising another bitterly cold night. She opened the door to see the genial face of one of the church's deacons, a farmer from out in the Valley.

"Mr. Matthews! Come in out of the cold," she said and stood aside while he entered the wide hall.

"Yes, Ma'am, thank ye. It's blowing up a bad one, I'm thinking. The parson in?"

"I'm afraid not," she answered. "He went to visit the Varners."

He bowed his head for a moment. "I heard about their boy. Sad thing, his truck sliding off the road like that, with the snowplow coming."

"Yes," she answered. "Won't you come in by the stove and warm yourself?"

"No Ma'am, better be getting on. The missus wanted me to bring you folks one of our sugar-cured hams." His face glowed with pride. The whole Valley knew about the delicious hams from the Matthews farm. He hefted the sack from his shoulder and laid it on the hall table.

"Why, thank you, Mr. Matthews. What a treat. We'll both enjoy it."

The farmer shuffled his feet and looked down at the hat he now held in his hand. "Ain't much, but I know the church ain't been able to pay the parson proper, seeing how the banks is closing and folks losing so much." He looked up and grinned at her. "But we intend to see that you don't go hungry. God's blessed us with good crops this past season, and," he glanced briefly at her, "well, we're gonna' take good care of you folks . . . the baby too." He blushed and turned to go.

Carolyn opened the door for him. "I know you will, Mr. Matthews. We've been blessed as well, by all of you good people." She smiled as he left.

He replaced the hat and headed toward his car, fighting the rising wind.

Carolyn stood for a moment watching the road, praying Jim was close to home. As she closed the door and turned toward the kitchen, she felt a painful cramp. "Oh!" she cried, and whispered, "hurry, Jim."

Before she could settle in her big rocker by the wood stove, she heard the welcome sound of the front door opening, and Jim's voice, "What's this, a ham?"

He came into the room just as another pain hit. She caught her breath and gave him a brave smile. "Yes. Mr. Matthews just brought it." She rose awkwardly to greet him, and he saw the pain in her eyes.

"Oh, Honey." He took her in his arms. "Is it time?"

"I think so," she said. "But how will you ever fetch Rosa in this weather?"

"I'll telephone John, and he can meet me halfway. It isn't far, just down to the Draft." He grinned. "Something told me to put those tire chains back on, this morning. Good thing I listened."

She winced again, and he said. "Now, let's get you to bed."

Twelve long hours later, Carolyn moaned from still another pain, and the nurse bent over her, wiping her forehead with a cool cloth. "Just a few more pushes, Mrs. Woolridge. I've delivered many a baby 'round these parts, but none as stubborn as this one." She chuckled as she moved to the foot of the bed. "It won't be long now. I can see the crown."

It was barely daylight when they heard the welcome wail of a newborn.

"Oh Jim," Carolyn groaned. *Where was he?*

Pacing the kitchen floor, Jim heard the cry, and headed for the stairs.

Rosa, exhausted but smiling broadly, met him on the stairs. "Come and see your daughter," she said.

In an instant, he was at the bedside. "Oh, Sweetheart, what a long, hard time you've been through." He discovered he was weeping as he bent over to kiss his wife.

"But look what we have here," she smiled and turned to the small bundle in her arms, as he sat on the bed beside her.

He stared in wonder as Carolyn put the tiny, squalling infant in her father's arms.

After a moment, the baby hushed, seeming to absorb the safety of her father's love for her. He looked at his wife. "I'd like to name her for my mother," he said reverently.

She nodded, as he handed the baby back. "Kate is a beautiful name." She uncovered the tiny feet and counted toes, then the fingers. "She's perfect, but she needs a middle name."

"You don't have one," he teased.

"I know, but I want her to have my sister's name. Augusta has her baby boy, but she might never have a girl."

"Then she's Kate Augusta Woolridge."

"Pastor, time for you to leave us. We need to get this baby cleaned up, and your wife is ready for some well-deserved rest," the nurse said.

Jim rose and kissed Carolyn once more. "I have some telegrams to send," he said, and left.

"Jim, it's been two weeks, and these wonderful meals are still coming in," Carolyn remarked as she nursed baby Kate in the big warm kitchen.

"These people love you," he said, unwrapping two hot casseroles and setting them on the table.

"They are the salt of the earth," she said, with a sigh. "I just wish they weren't going through such hard times, paying for the new church and struggling to meet expenses." She put the baby on her shoulder, and soon they heard a resounding burp. "She's asleep already," Carolyn said, laying the child in her cradle and joining her husband at the table.

After they blessed the food and the kind hands that had prepared it, Carolyn looked up at her husband. "I'm noticing that little 'worry-wrinkle' in your forehead, Jim. What's that about?"

"I don't suppose it's a worry," he said, forcing a grin. "But we do need to pray."

"Okay. Anything special?" she asked.

"I got a letter today from a church in Alabama. The same Presbytery where Rob is preaching. He and I talked last week about the difficulties the folks here are having, and the likelihood that they won't be able to pay my full salary any time soon."

"But Mama is glad to help with expenses, and you love these people. I love these people. I want Kate to grow up here in this beautiful valley." Her voice was almost pleading.

"I know, Honey," he said and laid a hand on hers. "I want that too, but don't you see? We're making it harder for them."

She was quiet for a while, as they ate. Then she said. "You're right. They want to do right by us, but they're all struggling in this terrible Depression."

"Exactly," he said. "The church in Uniontown needs a pastor. Rob gave my name to the Committee, and they wrote asking me to come down and preach a trial sermon, sometime next month.

"So soon," she whispered.

"I know. I told them I want you to go with me, and we need a little more time. They're willing to wait until the end of March."

She looked away. "It would be closer to Mama, and Augusta is moving home this summer."

"It's a half day's trip to Anniston, much closer than we are now."

As they finished up the chicken casserole, stewed apples and chocolate cream pie, Carolyn mused, "We'll never find a congregation as good to us as these folks are."

She rose and started clearing the table. "But I suppose we really do need to pray for God's will in this thing." She began filling the sink with water and adding the dishes. "He may be giving that Alabama pastorate to us---and to the people here." Even as she said it, the tears were starting.

Jim stood behind her and put his arms around her waist. "You're right, Carolyn. We'll never forget our first pastorate, but who knows what God has for us, in the Black Belt of Alabama?"

Chapter 29

LIFE IN THE BLACK BELT

The screen door slapped shut as Jim stepped into the coolness of the high-ceilinged hallway. Kate, now two and a half, ran to meet him, and he scooped her up in his arms.

"Did you have fun in the sand box this morning?" he asked, brushing sand off her bare toes and carrying her into the dining room.

"Uh-huh, and Miss Sadie helped me make pies, just like she makes," she said, scrambling down and going to her place at the table. He helped her into the high chair, and turned to kiss Carolyn, who came in at that moment.

Seated at the table while Sadie filled tall glasses with iced tea, he and Carolyn each took one of Kate's outstretched hands, and bowed their heads.

"Father, we thank Thee for all Thy blessings, for this day and the opportunity to serve Thee here in this town. We thank Thee for the food we are about to eat, and the hands that prepared it. In Jesus' Name, Amen."

"Sadie, you've done it again," Jim addressed the cook, who began to unload dishes from a small cart. "Fried chicken, creamed corn, field peas, biscuits . . ."

"And blackberry pie," she added.

"How can I get any work done this afternoon, after such a

feast?"

Sadie placed a steaming bowl on the table and said, "Law, Preacher, you just need a little nap and you'll be ready to go again." She laughed her deep belly laugh and headed for the kitchen.

Jim looked at Carolyn, picking at her food. "You still homesick for The Valley?" he asked, biting into a drumstick.

"I know it's silly, but I guess I am. We never had this stifling heat, and there was always a breeze." She patted her neck and arms with a linen napkin. "And I had a letter from Della Matthews this morning. Apparently, Finley Memorial is still struggling, because she talked about the preacher who comes from Mary Baldwin College every other week."

"Father," Kate broke in. "Did you see the mules?"

He looked at her. "The mules?"

Carolyn laughed. "She loves watching the wagons bringing the cotton to town. You should see her jumping to the rhythm of the mules."

"I didn't know mules had rhythm." He grinned at his daughter, as Carolyn spooned corn into her bowl.

"These do. There must have been eight or ten wagons going by this morning, all in a line. Kate thought she had to keep up with them."

"They were taking the first picking of cotton to the gin. Then it will be shipped by train, down to the coast," Jim said.

"Where did you learn all that?"

"Dr. Long was at the church this morning, and we heard 'your' mules. He told me they do this every summer. Guess we just didn't notice last year."

"Kate wasn't old enough to enjoy them."

Sadie brought the pie, and Carolyn began to cut slices for each of them, as Sadie removed dinner plates from the table.

Stopping by Carolyn's chair, she said, "You remember Miss White an' Miss Long coming to visit this afternoon?"

"Almost forgot," she smiled at Sadie. "Do we have some of your good sugar cookies to serve them?"

"Yes Ma'am. And I'm making fresh lemonade."

"You're a jewel, Sadie." Carolyn stood up and lifted Kate out of her chair, wiping her face with a napkin. "I don't know what I'd do without you."

Jim came around the table and kissed the top of Kate's head. "What do the ladies want to talk to you about?"

"The new officers for the Women's Executive Board, they said. It's time to prepare the slate for next year, so the new officers can go to Presbyterial training in September." She put Kate down and sighed. "But they'll probably have some juicy church gossip to pass on as well." She smiled sweetly at him. "They'll expect their pastor to come by and visit, I'm sure."

"I think I'm going to be busy at the church all afternoon. Got to get the bulletin information ready for Miss Hunter tomorrow."

"Coward," she whispered, but Kate heard her.

"What's a coward, Father?" she piped up.

He squatted down to answer her. "It usually means someone who is afraid of doing something scary, but," he cut a glance at Carolyn, "your mama was just teasing me."

"What's teasing, Father?"

He sighed. "Where did you get such an inquisitive mind?" He sat down again and took her on his lap. "We usually tease people we like a lot, saying things that might get a rise out of them."

Kate shook her head. "A what?"

Carolyn reached for Kate's hand. "Your Father is definitely not a coward, Kate, and don't you ever forget that, but," she glanced at her husband, "sometimes we do like to tease each other. Now, no more questions. Run tell Sadie 'thank you' for dinner, and then it will be time for a story and a nap."

When the swinging door closed, Jim said, "I have a Session Meeting tonight, been working on the agenda all morning. I dread it, after last month. We need to pray."

"I'll ask Sadie to keep Kate busy in the kitchen for a few minutes." She pushed the door open. "Meet you in the parlor."

𝕮𝖍𝖆𝖕𝖙𝖊𝖗 30

MEMORIES AND CHALLENGES
1937

"God is very good to you." Carolyn's elegant visitor spoke with a slight accent. Matriarch of the single Jewish family in Uniontown, Hannah and her relatives rarely visited in homes of the community. Carolyn had learned of her talent for making draperies, which the tall manse windows badly needed. So Hannah had been to the house often, bringing her skill and unique personality, as she fashioned draperies for the parlor.

Now she held Carolyn's newborn son, and gave him her blessing.

The November morning was warm, and Carolyn and her guest visited on the wide front porch. Serving a cool drink to the elderly woman, Carolyn felt a tear roll down her cheek.

"You are missing your dear mother," said Hannah, her deep, melodious voice full of compassion.

Carolyn blinked back more tears as she resumed her seat in the wicker rocker. "How did you know?"

"A mother knows these things," said Hannah quietly, lifting the baby to her shoulder. "You are thinking of how you long to tell her about this little one."

"Yes," murmured Carolyn, sipping her iced tea.

"She knows," crooned Hannah, nodding her head. "She

knows of God's blessing to you." She rocked a while and spoke again. "It has been a difficult time for you, these last months."

Carolyn sighed. "Yes." It was good to talk to someone who understood. "Having to leave Kate at the Heacocks', to go to the hospital in Selma. And the Cesarean section." She laughed a little. "You know I'm thirty-seven."

The old woman shook her head. "That is not old. I was forty when my Ibrahim was born." She shifted the sleeping infant to her lap. "And look at Sarah. She was nearly a hundred!" Hannah laughed softly.

"I know, but I had such a difficult delivery with Kate, and the doctor didn't want to take any chances. It's just that I am so weak and tired, even after three weeks. Jim tries to understand, but I'm afraid he's wanting his wife back, and Kate is asking to go back to the Heacocks' farm."

Carolyn's visitor smiled. "I saw Vera Heacock in the store yesterday. She told me about Kate's visit. Those boys of hers enjoyed having a little girl around. Sounded to me as if they all miss her."

After saying good-bye to her guest, Carolyn sat for a long while on the porch. Memories of the past months flooded her heart, and she wept, remembering her mother's funeral. *Dear Mama, how you enjoyed rocking Kate, and watching her learn and grow. And wouldn't you have been excited to hear the news about another grandchild? But you left us just days after I discovered it myself.*

The little family traveled to Anniston for the funeral. For several years, Augusta and her young son had been living with Annie in the big Victorian house where the two sisters grew up.

"Mama's heart had been failing for some time," Augusta told them as they sat around a table loaded with food brought in by church members following the service. Kate, after being

135

hugged by numerous friends of the family, had fallen asleep on the way home, and been placed in the antique baby bed in her parents' room. Her cousin Richard dozed in his mother's lap.

"Mama wouldn't go to the doctor, but sometimes, she'd get short of breath and have to lie down. She knew I was worried about how I would raise Richard alone, after his father died, and she didn't want to be a burden."

"That's just like Mama," Carolyn said. "What will you do now?"

Augusta took a bite of congealed fruit salad, swallowed, and answered, "I'm thankful to have a place to live, after the Depression, and with Henry gone." She smiled through sudden tears.

"But this house is so big. It was a wonderful place for us to grow up, but it's older now, and will need more upkeep." Carolyn looked around, and wondered out loud. "How will you manage by yourself?"

Augusta rose and carried her sleepy boy to his bed. Coming back to the table she said, "I'm thinking of making apartments, and renting them out. How do you feel about that, Carolyn? The house is yours too."

"Of course. And then you won't have to be here alone," Carolyn commented thoughtfully, as she refilled tea glasses. "How many apartments can you make?" she asked, taking her seat again.

"I'm thinking the upstairs would be one."

"Yes! There are two bedrooms and a bath, besides our old bedroom, and that's big enough for a combination living and dining room."

"I'll have to add a kitchen, in that big closet." Augusta's voice showed her excitement. "Then, our big old dining room downstairs here, and the little bedroom and bath, that used to be the servants' quarters, and the old kitchen can be redone."

Jim asked, "How are you going to manage all this?"

"Howard Michaels." She nodded toward Carolyn. "He's

Susan's brother. He's a contractor now. I can trust him to do a good job, and advise me. The papers are always advertising for rooms and apartments for wives and families of the servicemen out at the fort. I shouldn't have any trouble keeping renters."

Jim voiced another concern. "But you'll have strangers coming and going in your house."

"There's a separate entrance to the sleeping porch upstairs, and one on the side of the house, by the dining room. People wouldn't have to come through my rooms here." She paused, and added, "Dr. Kessler talked to me a few weeks ago, about working as hostess at the church. I didn't give him an answer, because I wanted to be home with Mama, but now . . ."

Jim spoke up, "That sounds perfect for you, Augusta. The salary, with rents from the house, should pay your expenses, even with the responsibility of raising a son on your own."

"He's almost six, and I want him to have a stable home and a church family. God is really looking after us. I've been praying about all this, and I believe we're going to be fine," she said as she rose to clear the table.

Two weeks after they returned to Uniontown, Jim came into the house waving an envelope. "They've accepted my application for that two-week study on Evangelism at the Seminary," he said.

Carolyn jumped into his arms and squealed, "That's wonderful!"

Suddenly Jim sobered. "But I don't see how . . ."

"Oh Jim, you must go! We've prayed for this!"

"But now you're pregnant, and there's no one to come and stay with you and Kate while I'm gone."

"You're right," Carolyn said, as she slumped into a chair. "I can't ask Augusta to come, with all the remodeling going on at the house."

"We'll just have to pray about this," Jim said. "I won't leave you alone here for two whole weeks."

The next morning Vera Heacock showed up at the front door with some early spring greens. "I thought you might like a good salad of this tender lettuce," she said.

Originally from the Mid-west, the Heacocks did not share the spirit of lethargy so prevalent in the town and church. The whole family, including two teen-aged boys, worked long hours at the dairy barn and in the fields. Vera's kitchen always smelled of fresh-baked bread and milk cooling in tall cans. Kate loved visiting there. She rambled the farm, played with the calves, and was generally spoiled by the whole family. Sometimes, when Mr. Heacock came in for his afternoon cup of coffee, she sat on his lap and had her own treat of "coffee-milk."

As soon as the ladies were seated in the parlor, Kate came running in.

"Miz Hiccup!" she cried, "Can I come to the farm an' play with the baby cows?" She plunked herself in a chair close to her mother.

"You can come any time your parents want to bring you," Vera said. "We miss having a little girl at our place."

The conversation soon began to bore Kate and she wandered back to the kitchen where Sadie was making pies for dinner.

"I'm so sorry about your mother, Carolyn," Vera said. "I remember the happy time we had with her on our picnic at the farm last summer. She was an interesting lady!" Vera laughed.

"Yes, and none of us knew she had a heart condition. We are very blessed that my sister has moved back to the family home, and could care for her, those last days."

Vera reached over and patted Carolyn's arm. "And how are you, my dear?"

Unexpectedly, Carolyn teared up. "I'm all right," she said, blinking back the tears.

Though several years her senior, Vera was the best friend Carolyn had in the church.

"No, you're not," she stated in her matter-of-fact Kansas

brogue.

That brought on the tears. "I'm sorry." Carolyn shook her head. "I guess I'm not." She tried to smile. "I'm pregnant, and Jim just got an invitation to a seminar in Richmond, and I can't call on my sister. She has her own problems right now. And Jim won't go and leave me alone for two weeks." She had to stop and wipe the tears away. "I'm sorry," she said again.

"There's nothing to be sorry about!" Vera went over and hugged Carolyn's shoulders. "You've just buried your mother, and your hormones are raging, I'm sure." She smiled. "I'm so happy about the baby, but I'll keep your secret. That's your news to tell, when the time comes."

She sat back down. "Now, what to do about this situation?" A grin lit her face. "The two of you can just move out to the farm for those two weeks Jim's gone."

Carolyn shook her head and said, "Oh, no."

Vera held up her hand. "You could come into town every day to check on the mail and things here at the manse." She stood up. "We'd love to have you! Since Rebecca went off to college, we have an extra bedroom, just for you." She started for the door and added, "It's calving season, and the men are at the barn all the time, except when they're hungry. I could use an extra pair of hands at the house."

Carolyn stood and tried again. "I can't just come and stay at your house. I don't want to impose."

She found herself enveloped in a hug. "You're not imposing. It was my idea. You need to be safe so Jim will go to his seminar and not worry, and Kate . . ."

They both laughed. "She'll be thrilled!" Carolyn said.

"Then it's settled. Tell Jim you're staying with us. He's to go to Richmond and never worry a minute about his two girls. I expect he needs this time away more than we know." She grinned. "Austin told me Session Meeting was less than congenial, again."

The decision made, Carolyn began preparing for the two of them to move to the farm.

The two weeks in the country were full of mixed emotions. It was the first time Jim and Carolyn had been separated, and she missed him terribly.

Kate was in heaven, playing with the newborn calves, riding on the shoulders of the boys, and generally being treated like a princess.

Time with Vera, preparing meals, doing laundry, and working in the garden were balm to Carolyn's spirit, as they shared family stories, recipes, and even some deep spiritual insights.

After they returned home, the morning sickness and fatigue set in, but Jim was home, refreshed and full of stories and ideas. As they prepared for bed that first night Jim rattled on about Seminary friends she knew.

"Remember Jason Wilkes?"

"The fellow with all the answers, big shot in the Synod of Virginia?"

"Yeah, he was our senior advisor at Seminary, and never got over a sense of his own importance." Jim grinned

"What's happened to him?"

"It seems he and his church secretary ran away together, just before Easter."

"How awful!"

"It was a big blow to his family, and to the church. His wife and kids went to her mom's home in Texas, I'm told." Jim was serious for a moment. "Funny," he mused, "no one seemed surprised. He was a large ego just ripe for trouble, I guess." Jim crawled into bed and Carolyn turned out the light.

"Even so," she murmured, "don't you get any ideas. I promise you wouldn't get away with that kind of thing."

She giggled as he took her in his arms. "Don't worry, Honey," he said, "I missed you way too much, these past two weeks, to ever jeopardize what we have."

One midsummer evening, as they walked with Kate pushing her doll carriage, he asked about her doctor's appointment that day.

"He wants me to see an obstetrician in Selma. He's just a family doctor, and new to the practice. He's concerned about my age, and the history of Kate's delivery." She glanced up at him. "He thinks I should go to the hospital in Selma and have a Cesarean Section."

Jim stopped and looked at her. "This sounds serious. Are you having any pain, any . . . trouble?"

She laughed and laid a hand on his arm. "No. Since the morning sickness let up, I'm feeling fine. It's just a precaution. He wants me to be in a large hospital, with an OB doctor."

"Then that's what we'll do," he said. And so they began to plan, as September arrived. Carolyn called her friend Vera. "I have another favor to ask," she said.

𝕮𝔥𝔞𝔭𝔱𝔢𝔯 𝟑𝟏

FINDING JESUS

The manse windows were open to catch the breeze. From the church next door, strains of "Savior, Like A Shepherd, Lead Us" floated on the air as Jim began the evening service. James was already asleep in his crib. Carolyn put Kate into the claw-foot tub with her toys and some bubble-bath. Happy to have this time alone with her mother, Kate rattled on about her friend Libby, her play house and her tall slide.

"Mama," she asked, swishing her hand in the bubbles, "Why can't I have some skates like Libby's got? I'm already four."

Carolyn picked up her daughter and wrapped her in a soft towel. "That's not quite old enough. You'll have skates when you're five, like Libby is."

Kate gazed past her mother's shoulder, at the lighted stained-glass window of the church. "Mama, who's that?"

Carolyn stopped toweling Kate's soft hair and said, "That's Jesus."

"He's holding a little lamb in his arms. It looks like my lambie."

"Yes," said her mother, sliding a soft pink gown over Kate's head. "That little lamb ran away and Jesus went to find it, because He loved it so much."

Kate crawled into her bed. "Like I ran away to Libby's

house?"

"Yes, like you ran away yesterday."

Kate snuggled under the covers. "And Father came and found me."

"Yes, he did."

"But Father wasn't smiling like Jesus."

"You're right, he wasn't. We were both worried about you. You disobeyed us, and you could get hurt, crossing the street without us."

"Is that why Father hugged me so tight?" Kate's voice was soft.

"Yes, Kate. Your father loves you very much."

"Just like Jesus?"

"Just like Jesus."

The next afternoon, as Kate was napping, Carolyn took baby James into the parlor where a large fan moved the warm air. She sat in the brocade rocker that had been Jim's gift to her when James was born, and settled the infant to nurse.

Sadie, dust cloth in hand, moved around the big room.

"Sorry your dinner was late," she said. "I had to send to the store for more milk for Miss Kate."

"Dinner was fine, Sadie, but I'm sorry you had to go to that trouble. I thought we had plenty left from Saturday's delivery."

"Yes Ma'am, but we sure ran out today."

Carolyn nodded. "That was Kate's fault. She turned her milk over not once, but three times, yesterday morning."

Sadie stopped dusting. "Why did she do that? She likes milk."

"I know, but not yesterday. It was frustrating. I was trying to get Kate ready for Sunday School, so Jim could take her, but she was really showing a stubborn streak." Carolyn shook her head.

"Wonder what . . ." Sadie muttered.

"She said she didn't want to go to Sunday School. Now, how would it look for the preacher's child to refuse to go to Sunday School?"

Sadie chuckled. "If Miss Kate sets her mind to something ain't no changing it."

"She's been fussing about Sunday School for weeks now, but yesterday was the worst."

Sadie took up her dusting again. "I expect I know about that," she said.

Carolyn shifted the baby to her shoulder. "What do you know about Sunday School, Sadie?"

"It's that teacher, I expect."

"The teacher? What about her?"

"When I cleaned for Miss Cameron last week, she told me she pulled her child out of Sunday School, keeping her home."

"Why?" Carolyn settled James on her other breast, and continued rocking.

"She says little Jeannette come from there crying, because that teacher rap that baby's knuckles with a ruler."

"Oh, Sadie, that's terrible. Why would she do such a thing?"

"Miss Cameron said because they didn't do the songs just right, so she punished them babies."

Sadie's countenance was clouded. She rubbed the piano top until it shone.

"As awful as it is, that explains why our Kate didn't want to go back there."

"Yes Ma'am." Sadie mumbled. Then she said, "That's a mean woman, Miss Woolridge. She's Dr. Long's old maid sister. She stayed in Birmingham for a while, some say she had a sweetheart that got away. She come back here in twenty-nine, been teaching the Beginner class ever since."

Carolyn got up and headed for the bedroom. "Something's just not right. I think my husband needs to know about this."

"Yes Ma'am," Sadie answered, flicking her dust cloth over a lamp, "I expect that's why Miss Cameron told me, but it probably won't do no good."

Two weeks later, on a rainy night, Jim opened the front door, and approached the bedroom, where a small bedside lamp lit a corner of the darkness.

"Carolyn," he whispered. "You asleep?"

She rolled over and sat up, patting the bed beside her. "Just waiting for you to come home." She looked at the china clock on the nightstand. "It's late. I thought this was just a meeting about Sunday School teachers."

"It was, but Tom cornered me, after the meeting. He needed to get some things off his chest." Jim sighed as he sat on the bed and began removing his shoes.

"Sounds like the Sunday School Reorganization plan didn't go over too well." She sighed. "Jane had such high hopes her husband could change some things, after all these years."

"Well, he got voted down at every turn. No new Sunday School teachers, no Planning Committee. I doubt he'll be Superintendent much longer. You know how the hierarchy works in this town. After all, their family's only been here eight years, and they're not related to the 'right people.'"

"But they love the Lord, and have such hearts to serve Him."

Jim's laugh was hollow, as he stood and began pulling off his tie. "You're right, but nobody listened to him, and when I tried to explain the possibilities for growth in the church, the good doctor looked at me and said, 'Preacher, we know what we oughta' do. We're just not gonna' do it.' And then he laughed!"

Carolyn reached out and took her husband's hand. "Oh Jim. I'm so sorry."

"I am too, Honey." He sat on the bed. "What do I do with that kind of attitude?"

As Jim undressed and pulled on his pajamas, she sat up and hugged her knees. "And Kate's Sunday School situation won't be changing," she said, with a sigh, then added, "You know, Jim, it almost feels as if we're living in the era of slavery, still."

He climbed into bed beside her. "Why do you say that?"

"Most of the people in this county seem to be 'owned' by one or two families. They live on someone else's land, buy from their stores, owe debts they'll never be able to pay."

He nodded, defeat lining his features. "It's a matter of power. I've finally figured out that's why nothing ever changes."

"It's more than that. It's a kind of fear. It's very deep." Carolyn's voice was heavy with sorrow.

He gave her a quizzical look. "Where did all this come from?"

"Jane and I talk about what we want for this town, for our families. Sometimes Vera Heacock joins us."

He smiled. "Your Monday morning prayer group?" He was quiet for a moment, thinking. "You all could be stirring up a hornet's nest."

"Your preaching, especially this series on John, is what's stirring things up. Changes are scary. People get hurt."

"Honey, I have to preach the truth."

"Of course, but . . ."

"The Gospel has been known to cause trouble, for centuries."

She nodded, stretching out under the covers.

Sliding in beside her, he said, "Honey, you know we need to forgive them."

"Humph," she responded, reaching to turn out the light.

After a moment she asked, "What was Rob calling about today?"

"A church in West Virginia. They're looking for a pastor."

Chapter 32

HIGHER GROUND
1938

Carolyn gazed out of the car window at the steep West Virginia mountain road and sighed. "Jim, I don't know if I can live here. I've never been this close to mountains. I feel a little claustrophobic."

He laughed. "You'll get used to it, Honey. Think of them as protective. After all, these mountains have been here, guarding this little town of Marlinton for a hundred years or more."

She wrapped her arms around herself. "But it's chilly, and this is July! How will I manage to keep the children from catching colds this winter?"

"Now you're borrowing trouble. They're gonna' love playing in the snow."

"Snow! I forgot about that! We'll have to buy them some warmer clothes."

They crossed the bridge and there, on their right, was the Presbyterian Church, a graceful brick building with a large maple tree on its sloping front lawn. "Want to stop and look at the church, or go on to the manse?" he asked.

"Let's go on," she said. "The children are both asleep, and I'd like a chance to look at the house before they wake up."

"Remember I warned you. It's bigger than the house in

Uniontown."

"I know. Two stories." Her brow creased with worry. "I miss Sadie already."

"We'll find someone to help with the house work, I'm sure." He patted her hand as they pulled up behind a large truck. "Well, our furniture is here. Looks like the movers are enjoying their lunch on our front porch."

"Preacher, the ladies are bringing supper over." The voice of Otis Smith, an elder and owner of the town's dairy, came across the telephone line. "Just wanted to be sure you were settled in." He hung up and Jim laughed as he made his way around boxes in the kitchen. "These mountain people don't waste words. Something we'll have to get used to," he told Carolyn. "That was Otis Smith on the phone, saying supper's on the way."

Carolyn put a restless, irritable toddler in his highchair, where graham crackers awaited his chubby hands. "They've already filled the pantry and refrigerator."

"Better clear some space on the table," he answered. "More's on the way."

At that moment, a high squeal sounded from the front of the house. Jim took off through the dining room. "Kate, don't . . ." But she had already discovered the joys of bannister-sliding, and his warning was too late.

He arrived as she bumped into the newel post at the bottom of the long staircase. He grabbed her up.

At the same moment, the doorbell rang. With a squirming Kate in his arms, Jim somehow opened the door and greeted three ladies standing on the front porch, arms loaded with wrapped dishes. The delicious aroma of roasted pork and apples assailed his senses.

"Good evening to you, Reverend Woolridge," said one as Kate slid from her father's grasp and disappeared. The woman who spoke was tall and wiry, with a slightly raspy voice and a thin smile. "Thought you might be getting hungry."

Jim opened the door wide, and mumbled a greeting as she sailed in, followed by the other two—one a large woman, and the other rather short.

"The kitchen . . ." Jim began.

"We know where it is," the tall one called over her shoulder. "We've been here before."

As they unloaded steaming dishes on the table, they introduced themselves, shaking hands with both Jim and Carolyn. "I'm Jane Bear," said the first. "I'm the telephone operator, so I'll soon know all your business." She laughed.

"And I'm Hazel Finegold," the large lady said. "My sister's husband is clerk of Session at the Church."

"And I'm Mattie Smith," said the third. "I play the organ at the church. And," she added, "my husband runs the dairy here. He'll deliver your milk in the morning." She approached the high chair. "What a beautiful baby," she said. James shook his golden curls and reached up sticky hands to her.

At that moment, Kate came into the room and stood by her father. Jim placed his hand on her shoulder and said, "This is Kate, our five-year-old."

"You are just the right age!" Hazel was on her knees, looking into Kate's eyes. "I teach the Primary Sunday School class, and we have a whole room full of boys and girls your size!" She laughed and clapped her hands. "We are going to have such fun!"

Kate's eyes grew wide, and then a big grin lighted her face. She'd never thought of Sunday School as *fun*.

That night, Carolyn came into the big upstairs bedroom after settling the children in their room next door. She sat beside Jim on the bed as he pulled off his socks.

"Still scared of the mountains?" he asked.

"A little," she answered, "but I think we can be happy here." She moved to the skirted dressing table and began brushing her hair. "Everything is different, but already I like these people."

Chapter 33

SNOW SUITS AND PARLOR WEDDINGS

October dressed the mountains in glorious color, and brought a new crispness to the air.

One Monday morning, Carolyn was staring at another mountain, the pile of dirty clothes in the middle of the kitchen floor. A hose from the sink's faucet was filling the washing machine as Zoolina, a tall, angular woman, pulled two large tubs from the pantry and set them on a bench. Carolyn loaded sheets and underwear into the washer, and then set it to work, while she filled the two rinse tubs, adding "bluing" to the second tub. An hour later, as she was pulling the last of the clothes from the rinse water and running them carefully through the wringer, she heard the screen door slam and Zoolina came in carrying a wicker clothes basket.

"A little chilly out there this morning, Zoolina?"

"Yes Ma'am, but the sun shinin'," she answered, a smile lighting her dark features, "we got room for one more load on the line," she said.

At that moment, the front doorbell rang, and a cry sounded from upstairs.

"I guess James is through with his morning nap." Carolyn dried her hands on her apron.

"I get the baby, and you better see who's at the door," Zoolina said as she headed for the hall.

"Zoolina," said Carolyn, pulling the apron over her head, "what would I ever do without you, especially on wash day?"

"Dunno,'" said the woman, heading upstairs. "Good thing Mrs. McGlaughlin don't need me so much, now her girls is growed up."

Carolyn hurried toward the front door, wondering who would come calling in the middle of a Monday.

She smiled as she saw her neighbor from up the street. "Greta! Come in."

"I know it's wash day, so I won't stay, but I just baked a batch of salt-rising bread, and wanted to drop off a couple of loaves on my way to the store."

Carolyn reached for the still-warm loaves, wrapped in a large linen towel. "We love your bread, Greta. Can you come and sit for a minute?"

As they settled in the living room, the older woman laughed. "You sound just like Minnie Pearl, on the radio," she said.

Carolyn felt her face grow warm. "I know. I wonder if I'll ever get rid of my Alabama accent."

"Oh, Dearie," said Greta. "Please don't worry about that! We all enjoy hearing you talk. It's just like listening to the Grand Ol' Opry, on Saturday nights." She laughed heartily.

"Well, I'm glad it makes people happy." Carolyn shrugged.

"And how are your children?"

"Oh, the baby just woke up, and Zoolina's changing him. Jim took Kate with him on an errand downtown. She loves being with her father. They stop and talk to everyone between here and Main Street."

Greta chuckled. "They're two peas in a pod," she said. "I do like seeing her standing there beside the preacher of a Sunday morning after church service."

"Greta," Carolyn said, "I'm a little worried about the winter. Does it get very cold here?"

Greta nodded. "Sometimes it gets down to ten or fifteen degrees, for weeks at a time, in December and January—even into February. 'Course, the kids don't mind, because they get to play in the snow, and sometimes the school closes, if the mountain roads get too bad."

Carolyn shivered a little. "How am I going to keep the children warm?"

Greta patted Carolyn's knee. "You just get yourself over to Mr. Briggs' company store, right across the river there. Get some cotton stockings for Kate to wear under her dresses, and snowsuits for both of them. Caps, scarves, gloves and galoshes, too. He just got all that winter stock in. I heard Etta talking about it at church yesterday." She paused. "And you better ask Silas, down at the drugstore for a big bottle of cod liver oil. A teaspoon a day goes a long way toward keeping children healthy. Your babies don't need to be catching any bad colds this winter." She got up and started toward the door.

Carolyn followed. "I guess I'm not prepared for a West Virginia winter. When do you think we'll have snow?"

"Some time around Thanksgiving, but we've been known to see snow as early as the end of this month, and it usually lasts through March."

"March! But the crocus . . . tulips . . . things begin to bloom in February."

Greta chuckled. "Not here, 'Minnie Pearl'. We dig in for long winters in these mountains. Don't see anything blooming 'til late April."

"Thanks for the warning," Carolyn said weakly.

As Greta approached the door, her voice became soft. "Just you wait 'til that first snow. Something really special about it. And when we get enough to cover the roads, Otis hitches his team to a great big sleigh, puts bells on the horses and picks up all the children for a ride around town." She smiled at Carolyn. "And, there's nothing like Christmas caroling in the snow, and hot chocolate in the church basement afterwards. Winter's not so bad. It's just long, some years." She was chuckling as she left.

When Jim and Kate came in the door, they found Carolyn

sitting in the rocker with James in her lap, looking as if she were about to cry.

"What's the matter, Honey?" he asked.

"Oh, Jim, I'm not ready to live in a place that's winter for half the year."

Later, as they ate vegetable soup along with thick slices of salt-rising bread, she reported what Greta said.

"Tell you what," Jim said. "You get the children settled for a nap, while I run Zoolina home, and make a visit across the river. This afternoon, we'll all go to Mr. Briggs' store, and outfit the four of us for a West Virginia winter."

That Saturday, just as the family finished lunch, the doorbell rang. Hoping the postman had brought a package or a catalog, instead of just letters for her father, Kate hurried to the front door.

On the porch she saw two strangers. A skinny, overalled young man held tightly to the hand of a frightened girl. "We . . . we wanta' see the preacher," the boy said.

Kate turned and fled to the kitchen. "Father, there's two people here that want to see you."

Jim smiled, swallowed a final drink of coffee and stood. "Must be the kids from over on the mountain." He went to the door and Kate heard, "Come in. Let's go in the living room."

Kate looked at her mother. "Who are they? What do they want to see Father about?"

Carolyn wiped James' hands and face and lifted him out of his high chair. She grinned at Kate and whispered, "I think they want to get married."

"Married! Here?"

"Shhh. Your father told me about a young couple who are part of the church where he preaches on Sunday afternoons, up on Droop Mountain."

Kate lowered her voice. "But why don't they just get married in their church?"

Carolyn sat down, taking James on her lap. "I think they're afraid."

Kate nodded her head. "They looked real scared, especially that girl. Why, Mama?"

"Your father told me that they belong to two families, both in that little church, who have been feuding for many years."

"What's 'feuding'?"

"Well, a long time ago, two cousins, named Winters and Summers, had a big fight over something—nobody can remember what it was—and their families have hated each other ever since. They go to the same church, but they never speak to each other, and there has been all kinds of trouble up there because of that feud."

"So why are those people here at our house?"

"The young man is part of one of the families, and she is part of the other." Carolyn's eyes sparkled as she continued, "they fell in love, and were forbidden to marry. So, I imagine, they sneaked away, came to town, went to the courthouse and got a marriage license. Now, they have come here so your father can marry them." Carolyn put James down and took dishes to the sink.

"How's he gonna' marry both of them?"

Carolyn laughed. "Your father will perform a wedding ceremony, right here in our front room, and they will be married."

"So," she said, applying a wash cloth to both children's hands and faces, "we're going to a wedding."

Minutes later, Kate stood beside her mother's chair. She and James didn't have to be told to be quiet. It felt like church, as they heard their father pray for the young couple standing before him. Then he opened a small black book and read,

The night has a thousand eyes, and the day but one,
Yet the light of the bright world dies with the dying sun.
The mind has a thousand eyes, and the heart but one,
Yet the light of a whole life dies when love is done.[1]

154

He looked up. "Dearly Beloved, we are gathered here today, in the presence of God and these witnesses," he said, smiling at his family, "to join this man and this woman in the holy bonds of marriage."

He asked them some questions, listened to their almost inaudible answers, and then said, "By the power vested in me by the Church of Jesus Christ and the state of West Virginia, I now pronounce you man and wife. What, therefore, God has joined together, let not man put asunder." He prayed again, and said to the boy, "You may kiss your bride now."

At that point, Kate thought she was going to die of embarrassment, but her mother was smiling through her tears.

1 Poem by Francis William Bourdillon

Chapter 34

THE WAR EFFORT
1943

"I got a bigger ball of tinfoil than you. I bet I can get in the picture show for free."

"Aw, Kendall. you don't know anything," Kate said as she climbed onto the picket fence in front of her house. "You gotta' pay a nickel to get in, even if you got a ball of tinfoil, or even a box full of tin cans." Waving her arms, she began walking the fence.

"Tat," James looked up at her with adoration in his large brown eyes, "why do we hafta' save up all that tinfoil an' stuff?"

Kate looked down from her perch on the fence rail, at her brother pulling his red wagon down the sidewalk.

"It's for the war effort, Dummy, just like Mama says. We gotta' save ration stamps and buy war bonds, so the army can get what they need to kill the Germans and Japs." Kate truly loved this sweet, curly-headed boy, but she wished he didn't have to hang around her all the time, asking questions.

"Well, I don't know why they don't just line 'em all up and shoot 'em, and be done with it," Kendall said, swinging on the lowest limb of the maple tree.

Kate jumped down and headed for the tree. "Here comes

Donnie. Let's play bomber airplane." She swung into the tree and scrambled to the topmost limb.

Minutes later, she heard her mother call, "Kate."

"Yes Ma'am?" she answered.

Carolyn was standing at the front gate, looking up. "Kate, what are you doing in the top of that tree?"

"I'm the airplane pilot, Mama," Kate yelled. "We're shooting down Germans and Japs."*

"Well, you almost 'shot down' the paper boy yesterday, with those rocks. No more rock throwing. And come down here right away."

Kate climbed down and jumped to the ground. She knew from the tone of her mother's voice that she was in trouble again, but it was so much fun playing with the boys, and she was the best climber, so she always got to be the pilot.

Carolyn assessed the damage to Kate's dress, and sighed. "Kate, you're ten years old. Why do you insist on being such a tomboy? I just finished letting down the hem of this dress so you can wear it to school, and you've torn it already."

Kate looked down at the small tear in the hem of the grimy dress. If she could just wear pants, like her brother, climbing would be so much easier.

"I'm sorry, Mama," she said, but she knew in her heart, that wasn't entirely true.

"Well, I need you to run down to Mrs. Thomas's store. I don't have enough bread for lunch, and you can get a small jar of peanut butter. Can I trust you to take this five-dollar bill and bring me back the change?" Carolyn handed her an envelope.

Kate's eyes got big. She'd never even held a five-dollar bill before. "Yes Ma'am," she said, brushing at the dirt on her skirt.

"Go get your little pocketbook, so you can put this in it."

The purse had been missing for days, ever since last Sunday, when she took it to church. "I'll hold tight to it, and I'll be real careful."

* Derogatory term for Japanese enemy, prevalent during World War II

"That's a lot of money. Mrs. Jackson just paid me for doing some typing for her. Be sure you don't lose it." Her mother's face wore that all-too-familiar frown of worry.

"I won't," said Kate, skipping down the sidewalk, the envelope folded tight in her fist.

Passing the bank, Kate met her friend Thelma, who lived uptown.

"Want to go look at the new dresses in Miss Lang's shop window?" Thelma asked. "My mama is thinking about buying me one for school."

"Sorry, I can't today." Kate lifted her chin. "I'm going to the store. I have five dollars." Maybe that would put a stop to Thelma's remarks about her hand-me-down dresses.

Kate breezed into the grocery store.

"Hello, Kate," Mrs. Thomas greeted her. "How is your mother feeling today?"

"She's better, thank you. The headache's gone."

"And what do you need this morning?"

"We need a loaf of bread and a small jar of peanut butter, please,"

Mrs. Thomas bustled around the store and brought the items to the counter. "Would you like a string of licorice?" she asked, putting the items in a bag.

"Oh yes, Ma'am!" Kate helped herself from the jar on the counter.

"That will be thirty cents," Mrs. Thomas said, as she pushed buttons on her cash register.

Kate reached for the bag, and opened her fist. She drew in a sharp breath. The envelope was not there. The money was gone!

She got down on the floor and looked all around. She spied two pennies and a sticky jawbreaker, but no envelope.

"Is something wrong, Kate?"

"Yes Ma'am . . .no Ma'am. Uh, can you put that on our bill, Mrs. Thomas?"

"Of course, Dear. Your father always pays his tab at the end of the month."

Kate took the bag and mumbled, "Thank you, Ma'am." She searched the floor as she left, and bumped into three people out on the sidewalk, as she looked around for the lost money.

All the way home, she scoured the sidewalk and the grass, even the street, but the envelope had vanished! Her heart turned to water at the thought of facing her mother.

When she came into the house, Carolyn was busy preparing lunch, and said, "Oh, Kate, there you are. I was beginning to worry." She took the bag from her daughter. "We need the bread for our tuna sandwiches." James was already at the table, gulping down his milk, and Kate could hear her father's voice as he came down the stairs from his study, singing "A Mighty Fortress Is Our God," a hymn he had chosen for the Sunday service.

She slunk into a chair, avoiding her parents' eyes. But her mother turned to her and asked, "Where's the change from the five dollars I gave you, Kate?"

Kate wanted to crawl under the table, because now both her parents were looking straight at her. "I . . . I . . . lost it," she mumbled.

"You LOST five dollars?" Her mother's voice was sharp. "How could you just lose that much money?"

"I . . . I don't know. When I got to the store, it was gone. I looked and looked, all over the store and all the way home. It . . . it's just gone," she wailed, and hid her face in her arms on the table.

Carolyn was close to tears. "That money was to buy shoes for school. I was up most of the night typing."

Jim, who had never raised his voice at the children, shouted, "Kate, how could you *do* this? Your mother trusted you. She worked hard for that money, so you children could have new shoes for school."

Kate fully expected her mother to send her to the backyard bush for a switch to use on her bare legs. Instead, in a voice filled with sadness, she merely said, "Go to your room for the rest of the day."

Kate rose, cast one glance at the sandwiches on the table, and climbed the stairs to the bedroom she shared with her brother.

Kate lay on the big white bed, her father's words ringing in her head. *Your mother trusted you.* Oh! It hurt so much, knowing that she had disappointed her parents. Would they give her away now, like her friend Joanne's parents gave her to those two old-maid aunts? She knew she should probably pray, but if her mama couldn't trust her, why would God even listen to her? As much as she hated the sting of the switch, she wished for it now. It only hurt a little while, and then Mama always hugged her and told her how much she loved her. She wondered if her parents would ever love her again. Desolate, she cried herself to sleep.

"Kate. Kate, wake up. It's time for supper, and I know you're hungry." *Was she dreaming?* No! It was her mother's sweet voice, and a kind hand was pushing back a strand of hair from Kate's face.

"Mama?" Kate mumbled.

"Come on downstairs now. Supper's ready."

Kate sat up. "Oh Mama, I'm so . . . ss . . so . . sorry." The tears were flowing again, and Kate found herself snuggled in her mother's arms.

"I am too, Honey." Carolyn took Kate's face in her hands and looked into her daughter's eyes. "It's a terrible thing to lose someone's trust. Now, you'll have to work hard to show us we can trust you again."

"Oh Mama, I'll do anything."

"It will take a while, and you'll have to pay back the money you lost. Your father and I have decided to keep your allowance in a jar, until all the money is repaid, except, of course, for your Sunday School offering."

"But that'll be a long time, and I can't go to the movies, or buy jaw breakers, or . . ."

"That's right. You'll have to give up some things until the

debt is paid." Her mother smiled at the sad look on Kate's face. "Of course, if you do some special chores for, say five cents, you might fill the jar up sooner."

"And you're not going to give me away, like Joanne's parents did?"

"Kate, that's one thing you don't ever have to worry about. You are God's gift to us. We love you very much, and we'll never give you away, no matter what you do."

That evening, Kate was quick to jump up and clear the table after supper. She didn't even argue with her brother, as they washed and dried the dishes.

Later, when they were sitting in the living room reading *Heidi,* they heard the terrifying wail of the air raid sirens. Jim came down the stairs, got his hard hat, a black box, and a flashlight from the hall closet, and left, warning them to pull all the shades and turn out the lights.

Shivering in the dark, Kate heard six-year-old James whimpering, as the frightening sound kept blaring. "Mama," Kate said, her voice trembling, "are the Germans gonna' bomb us, like in the newsreels?"

"No, Honey. Do you hear any airplanes? This is just a practice, to make sure our town is safe."

James' small voice trembled too. "Where's Father gone?"

"Your father is a warden, like many of the men in town. He has to go up on the mountain, where you two go for your picnics, to check and be sure there are no lights anywhere."

"What happens if he sees a light?" Kate asked.

"Did you see him pick up that black box? That's a walkie-talkie. He'll call the telephone office, and then Mr. Workman, the town policeman, will go and tell the folks to turn their lights off."

Carolyn opened a drawer on the small end table and pulled out a flashlight. Snapping it on, she said, "Let's go around the house and be sure all the shades are pulled down. We can march, like soldiers, but we must be quiet."

The children followed her through the dining room, to the

kitchen, where they pulled the shades on the two windows, then to the hallway, and the living room.

"Now," said Carolyn, "you soldiers follow me upstairs." It was hard, with just the small flashlight, but they held on to each other as Carolyn sang softly, "What a Friend We Have in Jesus." After they had pulled down the blinds in the study and front bedroom, they came to the children's room. After checking the blinds there, Carolyn announced, "We're going to play a game."

"In the dark?" asked Kate.

"Yes. In fact, that's the best way to play this game. Everybody on the bed."

The flashlight was turned off as they gathered on the big bed.

"We're going to play 'I Spy,' except it will be a little different. We'll say, 'I'm thinking of something.' "

"Can we give clues?" asked Kate.

"Yes, you can say, 'I'm thinking of something red, or soft, or sticky,' " said her mother.

"And the others hafta' guess what it is!" cried James, wriggling in his spot.

The game went on for half an hour, getting more and more exciting. They forgot to be afraid.

Suddenly, the sirens sounded again. The children crowded into their mother's lap. She laughed. "You don't have to be afraid. That's the 'all clear' signal."

Carolyn reached over to turn on a lamp. "Now, it's time for bed." She looked at her watch. "As a matter of fact, it's way past time. Quick, get your pajamas on, and run to the bathroom and brush your teeth."

"Can't we wait until Father gets home and see if he had to tell anybody to turn off their lights?" James whined.

"No," said his mother. "Your father won't be home for an hour or more. You need to be sound asleep by then." She scooted them off the bed. "You can talk to him in the morning."

A few minutes later, Carolyn bent to kiss Kate goodnight.

James was already asleep in his single bed by the window.

"That was fun, Mama. Can we do it tomorrow night?"

"It wouldn't be as much fun if we did it every night," Carolyn answered. "Let's wait until the next air raid drill."

Chapter 35

SHARING PAPPY

"The poor deacon was so scared he blurted out, 'M . . . m . . . marden me, Padam. You seem to be occupuing the wrong pie. May I sew you to another sheet?' "

The family was finishing lunch. They joined Jim as he howled with laughter at the story's punchline.

When he caught his breath, he said, rather soberly, "There's a lesson here, you know, about people who are full of their own importance."

"Like the lady who always sat in that pew, kinda' like Mrs. . ."

Jim held up his hand to stop his son's accusation.

"I'm sorry to say, there seem to be folks like that in every church." He looked at his children and said, "But I don't want you to be that way. Scripture says we are not to think of ourselves more highly than we ought to (Romans 12:3 NIV)."

He smiled. "Then there won't be any scared deacons getting their words all mixed up." He rose from the table as Carolyn motioned for the children to bring their plates to the kitchen.

"I like that story. I can't wait to tell Billy," James said as he put detergent into the dishpan.

"You'd never tell it like Father does," Kate needled him, stacking plates on the cabinet by the sink. "I think that's his favorite story."

"I kind of like the ones he tells in church, when he wiggles his eyebrows and looks like he's gonna' cry."

"Yeah, and Mrs. Sydenstricker always cries too." Kate picked up a glass and dried it, then declared, "Those stories kinda' make me sad."

"Aw, that's 'cause you're a girl, and you cry a lot anyway." James flicked soapy bubbles her way.

She responded by snapping the dish towel at his leg.

Carolyn, coming in with the last of the dishes, cut the battle short with, "Who wants to ride with your father to an auction sale up on Droop Mountain?"

"Not me. I told Billy we'd play ball this afternoon."

"I'll go, Mama!" Kate loved visiting those old mountain homes with her father. She met a lot of interesting characters, as Jim visited with the families gathered for these events.

"Wonder who's ringing the front door bell?" Carolyn said, turning toward the front of the house.

"I'll get it," Kate said, only too glad to put her dish towel down.

She flew down the hall and opened the door to a couple of teenagers. "Is Pappy at home?" the boy asked.

"Yeah. I . . . who?" Kate stared at them.

The girl smiled at Kate. "We're on the Synod Youth Council, and we just wanted to talk to him a minute about the Fall retreat."

The young man said, "Pappy . . . that's our name for your dad. He's kind of like a father to some of us." He grinned.

Kate didn't think she liked the sound of that, but she invited them to wait in the front room while she climbed the stairs to her father's study.

"Father," she said, approaching Jim's desk where he was typing. "There's some kids downstairs to see you about a fall retreat, or something."

When he stood, she asked, "Why do they call you 'Pappy'?"

Jim put his arm around her shoulders as they started toward

165

the stairs. "That's just because we work together on the Youth Council. I'm their advisor."

"But you're not their father."

Jim looked straight at his daughter, and saw the painful question in her eyes. "You're right, I'm not. I'm your father. It's just a name they made up, so they won't have to call me 'Mr. Woolridge.' " He gave her shoulder a squeeze and started downstairs.

Suddenly Kate felt sad. She didn't want to share her father with anyone, especially those Synod kids downstairs.

Weeks later, Kate entered the garage where her father was working at a table spread with cheesecloth, and holding two ham hocks. "Mama says supper's almost ready."

Jim finished rubbing one of the hocks with brown sugar and began to wrap it in the cheesecloth.

"Can I help?" she asked.

"In a minute. I'm about ready to hang up these hams so they can cure."

Kate straddled a sawhorse and waited. Finally, he looked at her.

"Okay, Tat," he said, using her brother's baby name for her, "let's hang these things up." She climbed onto the table and helped him lift the hams and hang them by their hooks on a chain looped over the rafters.

Kate remembered the horrible sight at the Barlow farm the day before. The pig shot in the head, strung up and sliced down the middle, blood flowing, the huge steaming pot on the outdoor fire, where they tossed the skin and fat, to render lard. She had hidden behind a woodpile and shut her eyes tight.

"These hams will taste really good in about six weeks," her father said, with a big grin. "And so will those pork chops your mama is canning, and the sausage she's put down in the crocks. The Barlows are good to sell us half a pig and butcher it for us." He began cleaning up the table, then brushed the sugar from his hands and jacket.

Kate asked a question that had been rolling around in her brain since Sunday. "Father," she said, "my Sunday School teacher says we're members of the *Southern* Presbyterian Church. What does that mean?"

Jim sighed. "It all started just before the Civil War. The country was divided, North and South." He looked sad.

The door opened on Carolyn and James. "Brr! It's cold in here, you two." Carolyn looked around. "I see you've finished with the hams. We're having tenderloin for supper."

Kate still had a question "Mama, what was the Civil War?"

Now her mother looked sad. "It was a war that never should have happened. Families were torn apart, especially here in West Virginia. So many died, and lost their family homes."

Jim put his hand on Kate's shoulder. "Back to your original question. When the nation split into North against South, so did most churches."

"Was that when the feud up on the mountain began?" James asked.

Jim laughed. "Maybe. No one seems to know."

"When we go to Alabama, the kids call us 'Yankees'. Are we?" James wanted to know.

"No" said his mother. "We are all Americans."

As they walked through the November dusk, Kate took her father's hand. "So, will the Northern and Southern churches ever get back together?"

"Perhaps. It's God's church, and He will direct our leaders to do what is best." He opened the back door and they trooped into the warm kitchen. "Meantime, our job is to faithfully preach the Gospel and bring people to a saving knowledge of Jesus Christ," he said as they headed to the sink to wash up

Chapter 36

SAYING GOODBYE

The children had been asleep for two hours when Jim came home that September night. Carolyn was waiting for him.

"How did the Session react?"

"They're good men, really sincere about asking me to reconsider the call. I almost changed my mind," Jim answered as he sat on the edge of the bed and pulled off his shoes and socks.

"Jim, we've prayed long and hard over this. It's time."

"I know." He shook his head wearily. "But they want me in North Carolina by December. It's a hard time for the church to lose a pastor."

"That's not your problem," she said. "That Executive Secretary job was offered to you because people in that Presbytery know you're more than a mountain preacher. That's why they wouldn't take your 'no' for their answer."

Jim hung up his trousers and jacket. "It does look like that ministry is what God has been preparing me for, what with the seminary courses I took last summer."

"When Davis and Elkins College gave you that doctorate last spring, I wondered what God had in mind for you. Now we know."

Jim sighed. "Still, I'll miss the pastorate."

"You'll be preaching, and shepherding church leaders."

Jim pulled on his pajamas and climbed into bed. "I know, and I'm excited about the challenges." He grinned. "Actually, I'm a little scared of the challenges." He pulled up the covers. "But I won't have to prepare new sermons for a while. I can dig into 'the barrel.' "

She turned off the bedside lamp and sighed. "These people have been good to us. Remember how we thought we'd never find a congregation like the people in Stuart's Draft? Well, these mountain folk come close, even if the Christmas Pounding did catch me off-guard every year."

Jim laughed. "It was always a great party and it filled our pantry for the year. These are good people, the 'salt of the earth.' "

"We'll need to tell the children tomorrow. Kate was so happy last week, when we told her you'd turned down the call, and that we weren't moving."

"It's a tough time for her, eighth grade," he said. "She barely remembers living anywhere but Marlinton."

"She'll bounce back. There will be tears, but she'll be okay."

"Time for true confessions. You really like the idea of moving back to the south, don't you?" he teased.

"You bet I do. Our lilac bush has only bloomed one time, in the eight years we've been here. I'm ready for some warm weather and a southern spring."

Chapter 37

NO MOUNTAINS HERE
DECEMBER 1946

Despite the happy smile on her mother's face, thirteen-year-old Kate was in tears as their train pulled into Raleigh's downtown station.

"Mama, I can't live here. They don't have any mountains!" she wailed.

Soon, however, Kate and Carolyn were caught up in welcoming hugs, as Jim and James met them.

"You look wonderful, Honey." Jim grabbed Carolyn in a fierce hug. "I really hated to leave you in that hospital and come down here with just James and the new puppy."

"It was hard to watch you two leave, but I was so sick with that awful pneumonia." She nodded at her daughter. "Kate's been such a help, staying with the neighbors and coming to the hospital every day." She gave James a big hug. "We're here now, and I hope we don't ever have to be separated again."

Thirty minutes later they entered their new North Carolina home, a brown-shingled cottage on the highway west of a small town named Cary.

"This is the only house for rent in the whole area," explained Jim as he carried suitcases around boxes in the tiny living room.

"It's cold. Where's the furnace?" Kate shivered as she looked around.

Her father smiled. "Right here." He patted a wood-burning stove in the center of the room. "This is the heating system. I banked the fire before we left." He opened a small door, stoked the fire and added wood from a nearby stack. "It'll be warm in a few minutes." He rubbed his hands together and turned to pick up Kate's suitcase. "You kids are upstairs, and we've borrowed a couple of electric heaters for you." He led the way up a set of stairs behind the kitchen.

Carolyn was busy unpacking bags. "It's late, and we're all tired. Get some sleep and tomorrow we'll go and visit the school."

"That's the reason I wanted to live in Cary," Jim told them. "The school here is excellent, better than ones in the Raleigh system, so I'm told."

"How far is it?" James wanted to know.

"About eight miles. You'll be riding a bus."

The next morning, Kate was awakened by her father's voice in the kitchen. "This stuff is awful," he was saying, as he held his coffee mug.

She scooted downstairs and ran into the bathroom, situated between the living room and her parents' bedroom, with a door into each room. Soon she came out.

"Yech!" she cried. "I can't stand to brush my teeth."

"It's the water," Carolyn said, a note of hysteria in her voice. "It's really hard."

"Stinks too," James contributed from the sink.

Despite the problems, the family soon settled into a routine. The children rode the school bus each morning and afternoon. Carolyn and Jim found bottled water and a softener product at a supermarket in Raleigh. The tiny house, with the additions of their cocker spaniel, Tarbaby and a stray kitten, made for close family times. At Christmas, the two-foot tall tree they found in the woods seemed to take up the entire living room, and the cry of "close the bathroom door," rang out whenever company came.

Then one cold, late-January day, Jim heard about a house for sale. Sitting on three acres, the home had been built by Mr. Sorrell, a Cary business man whose wife didn't like being "out in the woods." He had built her another house in downtown Cary, and was anxious to sell this one.

When Jim and his family walked through the front door, saw the fireplace glowing and all the room they could dream of— inside and out—they knew it was home. They moved in a week later.

Jim wanted to introduce the children to his step-mother's family in Oxford. And so, one February Saturday, they found their way to a rambling antebellum home near a country church in Granville County. Jim was to preach there the next day and the family, distant cousins, were their hosts. As snow swirled, a tall red-headed youth opened the farm gate for them, and they were soon welcomed by cousins Nat and Emmaline to a home warmed by fireplaces and lit by oil lamps. Kate slept in a feather bed, discovered what a chamber pot was, and washed her face in a bowl of icy water. She also fell quite ill—with a case of "love sickness", caused by the tall red head.

For the next two summers, Kate assisted her relative, as she held Vacation Bible Schools in the Presbytery's rural churches. Jim discovered that Emmaline had been a teacher in Johnston County twenty years earlier, and the people remembered her with great affection, so he asked her to serve a field which included five small, pastor-less churches. Kate gained an education which bore fruit over and over in her life. Being a guest in farm homes and teaching in one-room churches meant hot weather, outhouses, huge meals, and the uninhibited devotion of children who brought her bouquets of fragrant gardenias each morning.

Carolyn, released from the responsibilities of a local pastor's wife, settled happily into her southern home, the first house they had ever owned. As Jim worked with small mission churches, Carolyn became a mentor to the wives of the young pastors and elders Jim was training, and often invited them to her home. She also delighted in growing African violets in the sunny kitchen and dining room windows.

From Sorrell Street, they watched their town grow. Kate was involved in chorus and drama at Cary High School, and loved not being "the preacher's kid." Her father commuted to Raleigh just like all the other dads in town. James was a member of the school's young and struggling marching band, and had a paper route in the neighborhood. The family became charter members of a new Presbyterian church a few miles away.

Christmas always proved memorable. No more surprise "poundings", but the family were invited to Christmas parties at the country churches where Jim often preached. Kate and James were amazed at the tall, heavily berried holly trees that graced the small sanctuaries. Bags of fruit and nuts were always distributed to the children following the solemnly beautiful Nativity plays. Kate sensed, deep in her spirit, how much these hard-working farm families loved her father. "Dr. Woolridge" was indeed a pastor to these congregations.

In the car on the way home, the family always sang Christmas carols.

"Father," James spoke up between songs. "You forgot my favorite story when you preached last Sunday."

"The one about the boy and the wood pile?"

"That's the one. Don't know why I like it, 'cause I know you're talking about me."

Jim laughed. "It is all about proving your love for God by being obedient," he said, then added. "Sometimes you can use that lesson."

"I know, but I still like it."

Kate spoke up. "The one about God's love is my favorite, Father. But how can you be sure you haven't preached it twice in the same church?"

"Honey, you may have to get some new sermons," Carolyn said. "The children seem to have all your old ones memorized."

A week before Christmas, the family tramped through their woods, to find the perfect cedar tree to bring in and decorate as a fire roared on the hearth, and Carolyn prepared hot chocolate.

The family's Christmas Eve tradition continued. After attending a candlelight service at Raleigh's First Presbyterian Church, they gathered around the hearth. Kate and James hung up well-worn stockings, while Carolyn read "The Night Before Christmas." Then Jim read the Nativity story from Luke's Gospel and prayed, thanking God for the Gift of His Son at Christmas.

Later, when the children were in bed and she and Jim were loading the stockings with tangerines, apples, toothbrushes and small surprises, Carolyn said, "I wish Augusta and Richard could have come for Christmas. It will be lonely for them without any family in Anniston."

"Me too, Honey, but Augusta is really busy at the church this time of year. You'll enjoy your time with them in the summer, when the kids are out of school."

The hedge of roses was about to burst into bright color, while Carolyn's jonquils and hyacinths bloomed in the area by the little front stoop. It was a warm day in early March and Carolyn had invited two young pastors' wives for lunch. Sitting at her dining room table, mentoring these young women, Carolyn silently thanked God for the unique opportunity that was hers, as wife to the "Presbytery's Pastor."

While the ladies were enjoying coffee served in Carolyn's prized demitasse cups, Kate and James burst in. They had walked home from the school bus stop up on Reedy Creek Road.

Carolyn called them into the dining room and they both spoke to the company, before James headed to his room.

Kate was obviously bursting with excitement, so Carolyn

asked about her school day.

"We had auditions for the Senior play, and, Mama," Kate sang out, "I got a part!" She rushed on, "and we had a meeting about the Junior-Senior banquet, and the Glee Club is singing this glorious new piece, and I'm helping with the decorations, and . . ."

The ladies chuckled at her enthusiasm, and Carolyn said, "Slow down a little, Honey."

Kate, realizing she had rudely interrupted the party, began to blush. "I'm sorry, Mom. I just . . ."

Carolyn hugged her daughter, "I know. You've had an exciting day, and it looks like a busy time for you, right up to graduation."

As Kate headed to her room, she said, "By the way, Mama, I got the mail. It's on the kitchen table. We got a letter from King College."

Each August, the family attended the Home Mission Conference in Montreat, the Southern Presbyterian Church's center in the Blue Ridge mountains. One afternoon, after a long day of meetings, Jim suggested that he and Carolyn "escape" to Asheville for dinner. "Kate and James are at the skating rink with their club program, and I need to talk to you," Jim said as they walked up the mountain trail to their rented cottage.

Over dinner, Jim shared that he had been approached about a pastorate. "After six years as Executive Secretary, I find I have a yearning to be back in the pastorate," he told her.

"Where . . . when would we be moving?" she asked, wondering how she could give up the home she loved.

"Not until spring, or early summer. We have Stewardship Season coming up, and then Christmas, and several pastors to interview and train for ordination."

She was thinking out loud. "It wouldn't bother Kate much. She'll be a sophomore at King. But James will be looking at his senior year in high school. That might be hard," she said. "What brought all this on?"

"This morning, I talked with a fellow from Harmony Presbytery in South Carolina. They have a church that needs a strong pastor," he said. "They've had some trouble keeping pastors. The leadership is difficult, I understand." He grinned.

"And you want to jump into that situation?"

"I think I'm up for the challenge. That is, if the Lord is calling us there."

Chapter 38

HOME TO HARMONY
1953

Midday heat shimmered on the sidewalk as Kate got off the bus and jumped into her father's arms. Soon, he had stowed her two heavy bags in the car and they were on their way down Bishopville's main street.

Pulling into the driveway beside a large, white-columned house, Jim said, "Welcome to South Carolina, Kate."

She stared at the antebellum-style house, then let her gaze roam to the hundred-year-old brick church across the lawn, shaded by the largest magnolia she had ever seen.

As she got out of the car, she heard ferocious barking. A black blur flew around the side of the house. "Tarbaby!" She bent down. "I'm glad to see you too." Kate laughed as she rubbed the soft head and silky ears of the cocker spaniel who planted her paws on Kate's shoulders and licked her face.

A voice boomed from the front porch, where a tall black man, carrying a chair under each arm, asked, "You want these here chairs up on the piazza, Missus?"

"Who is that?" Kate asked her father, noticing that her mother had opened the front door and ushered the man inside.

Heading toward the house with the suitcases, her father answered, "That's Jake. He's the church custodian. Good as gold, but deaf as a post since he was a teenager."

"How do you communicate with him?" she asked, following Jim up the porch steps.

"He carries a pad and pencil in his shirt pocket. We write notes." Her father laughed. "I find myself shouting for him all over the church. Whole lot of good that does."

The screen door was flung open and Kate was suddenly enveloped in her mother's arms. "Welcome home, Honey!" she cried, as Jim passed her with the suitcases.

"Your room's ready, just follow your father upstairs," Carolyn said, and turned toward the dining room. "Dinner will be ready soon."

"Dinner in the middle of the day?" she asked as they entered the upstairs hall.

"That's the way they do it here. Dinner at noon, and I still don't know when supper is."

A slight breeze, stirred by an electric fan, fluttered organdy curtains. The white bed and dresser of Kate's childhood welcomed her.

"This room is huge!" she said, as Jim deposited her bags.

"A little larger than your dorm room." He chuckled and walked toward an open door. "You and your brother will share a bathroom. His room is on the other side."

"Where *is* my little brother?"

"At the high school, practicing with the band for tomorrow's graduation. It seems that, when he went to register for next fall, the director grabbed him and his trombone, for the program."

"Mama wrote that he was going to Transylvania Music Camp in a couple of weeks. I know he really wanted to get a spot there."

"Yep, and he's life-guarding to pay his way."

Kate noticed another door. "What's in there?"

"The sleeping porch, or, as Jake calls it, 'the piazza'. My study is across the hall." Jim gave his daughter a hug. "Glad you're home, Tat. I have a couple of things to 'tend to over at the church. See you at dinner." He was down the stairs and gone.

Kate checked out the porch, where two chairs and a cot stood. She noticed an outside stairway, and Jake's back, as he loped across the lawn to the church. The rooms were warm and stuffy, but what luxury, to have all this space to herself, and share a bathroom with only one person! She'd have to get used to that, and to having dinner in the middle of the day.

On her way down the graceful, winding staircase and into the high-ceilinged entrance hall, Kate thought, *what a great place to have a wedding. S*he followed her nose to the kitchen where a tiny woman was standing at the stove stirring a pot, and her mother was retrieving a large covered dish from the refrigerator. Kate glanced out through the small screened porch, to see sheets billowing from a clothesline in the back yard.

Carolyn looked up. "Hi, Honey. Where's your father?"

"He said he had a couple of things to do at the church, and would be back for dinner."

Her mother sighed. "When Gabriel blows his horn, your father will have to go by the church first." Kate grinned at the familiar complaint.

Carolyn turned to the cook. "Sarah, this is my daughter Kate, home from college for the summer."

Sarah ducked her head. "Pleased to meet you, Miss Kate," she said, and turned back to stirring the gravy.

Kate followed her mother into the coolness of the dining room. Setting the dish on the table, Carolyn said, "We've been here almost a month, and these people are still bringing food. Look at this lovely congealed salad Mrs. Higgenbottom brought this morning. And Mrs. Quarrels brought an orange chiffon cake by yesterday. They both said they wanted to welcome you to Bishopville."

Lowering her voice, Carolyn answered Kate's unasked question. "Sarah 'comes with the manse', I tried to explain to the church ladies that I really don't need any hired help, since you and James are both grown, but they insisted, so Sarah's here two days a week. She's an excellent cook, and has been a big help with the unpacking."

"Does she do the ironing too?" Kate asked, thinking of the full skirts and petticoats in her suitcases.

Her mother smiled. "Oh yes. You won't have to iron your father's shirts this summer."

"What will I do with all my time?"

"I think your father has plans for your time," Carolyn said, as she arranged plates and silverware for the meal. "There's to be a two-week Vacation Bible School, and he's volunteered you to teach the Primary class. There's also talk of a VBS at Smith Memorial, a small Negro church on the other side of town."

"I guess I should get my drivers' license, too, since I'll be graduating in a couple of years, and going to work."

Her mother took a vase of peonies from the sideboard and placed them in the center of the table. "Oh, you can just run down the street, to the license office behind the Court House. I got mine renewed there last week." She grinned; a bit embarrassed. "I almost flunked the test."

"Mama, I can't believe that. Didn't you have a South Carolina Drivers' Manual?"

"Of course I did, but they had all this stuff about drunk drivers in there. I knew I wasn't going to be drinking, so I didn't bother to read that part. And do you know, they asked questions about that?"

Sarah's soft voice interrupted them. "Ma'am, I got dinner ready."

"Wonderful! I'll call Mr. Woolridge." But before Carolyn could get to the telephone on the hall table, Jim came in, slamming the screen door and yelling, "He can't do that!"

Carolyn met him in the living room. "Who can't do what?" she asked.

"The clerk of Session."

"What's he done?"

"I've been searching all over for Session records, so they can be reviewed by Presbytery next week. Finally, my secretary confessed that the clerk always polled the Session members when anything needed to be decided. They never met! They never took minutes, so there are no records. Anywhere."

"How could he do that?"

Jim slumped into a chair. "Angela says he told each member that all the others were voting a certain way, and they always agreed." He shook his head. "No wonder people are afraid of him. He's running the church, and the county, with an iron hand."

"You're right, Jim." Carolyn said as she put an arm around his shoulders. "He can't do that."

Jim nodded. "It's not his church. It's God's church."

As Sarah brought a platter of roast beef to the table, Carolyn leaned over to kiss her husband's cheek.

"I think you have your work cut out for you, here in *Harmony* Presbytery."

Chapter 39

TARRED AND FEATHERED

The afternoon was hot and muggy. Kate and Sharon Bunting packed story papers, art supplies, Bibles, and pictures into Sharon's station wagon. They were on their way to Smith Memorial, on the other side of town.

Hefting a huge box of Bible Story books, Kate said, "Where's my brother, when we need him to help with all this? Out in the mountains where it's cool."

"I think it's great he was invited to Transylvania for a second summer."

Kate placed the box in Sharon's trunk. "Your Sunday School class really came through for this Bible School."

"Yeah," Sharon replied, stowing bags of pens, markers, pencils, glue and scissors. "It all started last summer—when you first got involved." She smiled at Kate. "We'd been wanting to help with something really important, ever since your mom began teaching our Young Adult class. We heard that they never had a Vacation Bible School at Smith Memorial, and decided we'd add to the materials left over from our church's VBS, and take it over there." She climbed into the driver's seat. "We didn't know much about what we were doing last year, but this year lots of church people have come through with offers to help. The kids are going to love having all this stuff." She grinned at Kate. "And aren't you lucky you get to help, again?"

She sighed as she pulled the car door shut. "We got by with it last year, but it could be a different story this time. My husband says some of the church leadership are not happy about what we're doing."

Kate settled into the passenger seat, and replied, "Well, they'll just have to get over it."

Arriving at the one-room frame building, they were greeted by Pastor Shelby and several women, surrounded by children of all ages. Soon classes were set up in both ends of the building, with the older children meeting under a shade-tree in the front yard.

While Sharon played "Onward, Christian Soldiers" on the ancient upright piano, the children filed in for the opening ceremony. Beginners and Primaries sat on one side of the aisle, Juniors and Youth on the other. Short legs dangled from the wooden benches, and paper fans flapped in the humid air.

Pastor Shelby stood up. "Let us pray," he said, and every head bowed. "Oh God, Thou Who art Infinite, Eternal and Unchangeable, in Thy Being, Wisdom, Power, Holiness, Justice, Goodness and Truth . . ." he began.

Two hours sped by. Mothers served lemonade and cookies, after the classes were dismissed. Kate was packing up papers and pictures when she heard music coming from the front yard. Saundra and Lizzie, two of the older girls who taught the Beginners, were singing, in pure, golden harmony,

> Jesus, Keep Me Near the Cross.
> There a precious fountain,
> Free to all a healing stream,
> Flows from Calvary's mountain.

They were joined by others, until the music pulsed across the dusty yard and rose like an anthem on the evening air,

In the Cross, in the Cross
Be my glory ever,
Till my raptured soul shall find
Rest beyond the river.[1]

Kate's heart felt ready to burst. Along with the loving hugs of bright-eyed, pig-tailed girls and mischievous small boys, to hear music from the hearts of these people lifting heavenward was the purest worship she had ever experienced.

The week ended with more food than Kate had ever seen spread on tables under the trees, and more singing. As Pastor Shelby closed the VBS program in prayer, Kate knew they had all been very close to heaven.

They had also been close to trouble. On the way home, Sharon mentioned that an emergency meeting of the church's officers had been called for the next Monday night.

"What's the matter? All we did was teach children about Jesus. Isn't that what Christians are supposed to do?"

"Apparently not *those* children," Sharon answered, her voice quivering slightly.

The next evening, Kate, reading in the living room where a breeze came through the open window, overheard a conversation between her parents.

"Jim, what's going on?" Carolyn asked, as they sat on the porch swing. "Mrs. Higginbotham dropped by this morning with a bowl of dahlias, and had a lot of questions about what's happening at Smith Memorial. I didn't tell her you've been teaching a Bible class there all these months, or about the Vacation Bible School. But she must have heard something."

"Yes, some of the Session members–you know which ones–got wind of that, and delivered an ultimatum."

"How dare they? What did they say?"

1 Words by Fannie Crosby. Presbyterian Church Hymnal

"It seems that I have plenty to do here at First Presbyterian, and they want me to curtail my relationship with that group–they don't even call them a church–and its pastor."

"Why? What is the harm?"

"They're scared, Carolyn. We've all heard talk of civil rights rallies in Alabama. The Negro population in our county is far greater than the white population. The white leadership can't control these people forever. I think they know that, and they're afraid of what could happen once this civil rights thing gets started and spreads across the South."

"But Pastor Shelby, his congregation . . . they're gentle, good people."

"Yes, they are, but they have never been treated fairly, and times are changing. Lots of white folk are getting very nervous."

"What should we do?"

"Just what we've been doing. Rely on the Lord and keep serving Him. He's never failed us yet."

As they entered the house, Kate heard her mother say, "What are you thinking about the letter from North Alabama?"

"I can't consider that right now."

The July Sunday dawned hot and sultry. Kate was awakened by her father's voice. Still in her blue baby-doll pajamas, she crept downstairs to see what had made her father raise his voice.

"Don't you ever come to my *back* door again! You are a minister of the Gospel, just as I am," he roared.

Kate peeped into the kitchen. On the doorstep stood Pastor Shelby. Kate knew he lived and worked in Florence and rode the bus to Bishopville twice a month, to minister to the congregation at Smith Memorial.

The screen door swung wide, and Kate ran for the stairs as Jim led his guest to the front porch. Later she heard their laughter, and snippets of conversation, as this humble man and the pastor of First Presbyterian Church sat in plain sight, on the manse porch, enjoying each other very much.

Kate wondered, as she slipped on her white, dotted-Swiss dress and combed her long brown hair, what the future held for her family and the church.

The next afternoon, as Kate came into the house after work, she heard her mother scream. "Poor Tarbaby!" Carolyn sobbed out, "Who would do such a thing?"

"I know who," her husband said through gritted teeth and headed out the screened door.

It was then that Kate, entering the kitchen, saw the lifeless body of their beloved pet on the bottom step.

The next Sunday, the family gathered in the dining room for breakfast.

As Jim pulled out his chair and sat down, he announced cheerily, "We'll know after the service today whether we'll be moving to Alabama to live with your Aunt Augusta." He stretched out his hands, for the blessing. "Let's thank God for this beautiful Sabbath day, and for your mama's good breakfast."

Suddenly Kate remembered hearing the late-night knock on the door. In the same way she and James had done as children, she crept halfway down the stairs to listen to the tense conversation in the living room.

She heard her father say, "No, John," as he spoke to the deacon who stood with him in the living room. Kate recognized his voice—he was Sharon's husband.

"I know you are our friend, and mean well, but . . ."

"Please, Pastor, for the sake of your family. I beg you, leave while you can. You don't know them. They're powerful, and they mean to run you out of town, one way or the other." His voice rose in intensity. "They've done it before."

"I know that, John, but God is more powerful." Kate moved down a couple of steps, so she wouldn't miss a word. Her father continued, "That faction has ruled the church, and the county, too long. That's why this church hasn't grown, why it has no impact on the community. Your family and other members of our Young Adult Sunday School Class are making a difference. We are about to become the church of Jesus Christ, here in Bishopville."

"But, Pastor . . ."

They were moving into the hallway. Kate scooted up the stairs, as she heard, "Thank you, John, for your concern, but I am not leaving this church until God sends me somewhere else."

At the table that Sunday, Jim explained. "Presbytery meets next week. A few members of our Session are circulating a petition asking that pastoral relations be dissolved.*"*

He grinned. "That means I could be 'fired' from the church. Presbytery will decide." He took a drink of his coffee and went on, "The Congregational vote happens today, following the sermon."

He picked up a forkful of his poached egg and toast. "Are you staying for the vote?" He asked them, his eyes twinkling.

Kate wondered how her father could be so calm, so unconcerned about this, when all their lives were in danger. "We might be homeless by this afternoon!" she wailed.

"No, we won't." Carolyn spoke up. "Augusta says we're welcome to move into the big house in Anniston."

"But, what about James, and me, and college? How will we . . . get along?" Kate was thinking of her summer job at the County Extension Office, and plans for her senior year and graduation.

"All that's in God's hands," said her mother. "Your father is following God's leadership, and we can trust Him to work everything out for His purposes and our good."

Suddenly, the pastor was serious. "I know this is all pretty scary, Kate, but it's a great opportunity to completely trust

God." He smiled at his daughter and continued, "You know, He sent us here in the first place."

"What are you preaching about?" Kate wanted to know.

"Your favorite sermon, 'The Love of God' ", Carolyn said.

Chapter 40

THE VOTE
1954

The church was packed. The air, even with fans whirring, hot and stuffy.

Jim stepped to the pulpit and opened his Bible to the First Epistle of John. He read, "Behold, what manner of love the Father hath bestowed upon us, that we should be called the sons of God."(I John 3:1a KJV) He flipped to John 3:16. "For God so loved the world that He gave His only begotten Son, that whosoever believeth in Him should not perish, but have everlasting life."

Looking up, he gazed for a moment at the upturned faces of his congregation, remembering sickbed prayers, funerals, marriage counseling, hearts poured out in shame and sorrow, joy and tears.

"I want you to come with me to a skull-shaped hill, on the darkest day in human history. There three crosses are raised, and God's own Son is dying in agony, so that you and I, ruined by sin, can be forgiven. So that," he glanced down at the Scripture, "we might be called 'the sons of God.' " As he proceeded to illustrate God's love in one story after another, many in the audience swiped at tears, but only Carolyn knew, by the faint twitching of his eyebrows, how Jim struggled to control his own emotions. When he finished, he announced a hymn. The organist began to play and the people stood to sing.

> Come ye disconsolate
> Where'er ye languish.
> Come to the mercy seat,
> Fervently kneel.
> Here bring your wounded hearts,
> Here tell your anguish;
> Earth has no sorrow heaven cannot heal.[1]

Still standing, the people received the benediction as Jim raised his hand over them. "The Lord bless thee and keep thee: The Lord make His face shine upon thee, and be gracious unto thee: The Lord lift up his countenance upon thee, and give the peace. Amen." (Numbers 6:24-26 KJV)

Asking them to be seated, Jim called the Congregational Meeting to order and led in prayer. He introduced the clerk of Session, who read the petition to Presbytery, requesting dissolution of pastoral relations between First Presbyterian Church of Bishopville, South Carolina and the Reverend James Woolridge.

For a moment, no air stirred in the sanctuary. Then a meek voice made a motion to send the petition to Presbytery. A barely audible "second" followed, and the clerk called for the question. Three voices voted "Yes", and the congregation, suddenly jumping to their feet, voted a resounding "No!"

"Motion is defeated." the clerk said, just above a whisper. Then he walked up the aisle, lifted his hat from the rack in the vestibule, and left the building.

Jim entertained a motion to adjourn, and closed the meeting with prayer. As soon as they heard his "Amen," the people surged toward the front to embrace their pastor and his family.

1 Hymn by Thomas Moore, Presbyterian Church Hymnal

That afternoon, Jim left the house for an hour. When he returned, Carolyn and Kate were on the front porch. "Where did you go?" Carolyn asked.

"I told you I had a call to make." He sat beside her in the swing. "I went over to see Tom," he said, referring to the clerk of Session.

"Why?"

"He suffered a heavy blow this morning. It's the end of an era, the loss of his power in this town." He looked at his wife, deep sadness in his eyes. "He's a broken man, Carolyn, and it was all so unnecessary."

"Anyone want some lemonade?" asked Kate, jumping up and heading for the kitchen.

Carolyn took her husband's hand. "Now will you think about talking to the people in North Alabama?"

Chapter 41

PASTORING ANOTHER PRESBYTERY

Christmas music filled the house on Dunlap Street in Guntersville, Alabama.

Carolyn sang along as she cut up oranges and grapefruit for ambrosia. Adding shredded coconut and a few cranberries for color, she covered the cut glass bowl and set it aside. She checked on the turkey tetrazzini in the oven, and headed to the dining room.

A red damask cloth covered the table, with greenery and a golden ribbon forming a centerpiece. On the living room mantle red candles nestled among greenery and Carolyn's collection of china angels. Four stockings were already hung. Under the front window, a table held the family's Nativity scene, complete with the Holy Family and animals collected over the years. Santa, in a wooden sleigh pulled by reindeer candles, graced Carolyn's small desk in the hall. In the carport a fir tree, purchased from the Boy Scouts, waited for the arrival of Kate from her job in Virginia, and James from Davidson College.

Jim and Carolyn were expecting guests for lunch, four young pastors and their wives. As Executive Secretary of North Alabama Presbytery, Jim had mentored these men and their small congregations. Carolyn enjoyed getting to know the young men, as she served them coffee and occasional lunches, when they met with Jim at the house.

As Carolyn set gleaming silverware at ten places, she glanced at the delicate rose-patterned chocolate set on the sideboard, a treasured gift from her Young Adult class in Bishopville. She remembered the November evening, just over a year ago, when they said goodbye to the class and other dear friends in the church. Tears flowed as they hugged Sharon and Bob, along with other couples who had grown in their faith under Carolyn's teaching, and become close friends. But their ministry at Bishopville's First Presbyterian was finished. It was time to move on to another charge.

Jim, coming downstairs from his office, sniffed the air. "Something smells good," he said, lifting the lid on the pot of green beans and eyeing the applesauce cake on the kitchen table.

"No taste-testing," Carolyn said, walking into the kitchen.

"Just got off the phone with Samuel Stone. They're coming!"

"Oh, I'm so glad. When I talked with Phyllis, she wasn't sure about the baby-sitting situation."

"Samuel's parents are there, for the ordination, so they're happy to take care of the baby."

"That's going to be a big celebration!" Carolyn reached into a cabinet, pulled out a bread basket and lined it with a Christmas napkin.

Jim sneaked a cream-cheese-filled celery stick from a silver tray on the table. "It's going to be even bigger than we thought. We're having a baptism."

"Oh Jim, that's wonderful."

"AND Samuel asked me to do the honors." Jim's grin spread across his face.

"I hope it all goes well for them."

"Honey, you worry too much. True, some of the brethren still think all black pastors should belong to Snedeker Memorial Synod . . ."

"That's ridiculous!" Carolyn said, sliding the rolls into the oven. "They're right here in our Presbytery, and they've worked hard to build that little church, with a beautiful congregation of both races worshiping and working together."

"We'll have a solid quorum of men who feel the same way we do. As you said, it's going to be a big day. Sunday will be here before you know it."

"And," said Carolyn, glancing at the clock on the stove, and untying her apron, "our guests will be here before you know it. Better get your tie and jacket on."

Chapter 42

FINALLY HOME
MARCH, 1961

Warm spring sunshine beamed through the kitchen window. Carolyn waved at Jim as he filled the wide shelf that served as a huge bird feeder, drawing wrens from their nest under the eaves, bright cardinals and saucy black-capped chickadees.

"Still a little brisk out there," Jim said, hanging his flannel jacket in the hall and coming into the room, "but spring is definitely in the air."

"I know," Carolyn grinned as she poured his coffee. "The daffodils along the driveway are in full bloom already."

They were finishing up oatmeal and wheat toast, when the back door opened and a short, sweet-faced, woman appeared.

"Good morning, Sophie," Jim said, rising. "Come and join us."

"No, Mr. Woolridge, I better get on upstairs and start my cleaning."

"That can wait. We're about to have prayers and you know you're welcome to join us." He pulled out a third chair as Carolyn poured a cup of coffee and set it on the table.

After praying for their children, three grandchildren, missionaries and pastors on their list, Jim got up. "Got an appointment with Dr. Allenby this morning." He started for the stairs, commenting as he went, "I want to get some things ready to take to the Post Office when I go downtown."

"Tell him I'm keeping you on your diet," Carolyn called after him as she started clearing the table.

She had just finished the dishes and was watching the hungry birds when Jim came back downstairs. He walked into the kitchen and, as he often did, put his arms around her and kissed the back of her neck.

"I'm a lucky woman," she murmured, as he left.

He walked into the dining room, and she turned her attention back to the window.

In the next instant, she heard a "thud" and ran to the next room, calling, "Jim!"

He lay face down on the floor. He never heard her voice.

Sophie, running in, gasped at the sight of Carolyn kneeling beside her prostrate husband. "Please, Sophie," Carolyn choked out, "call Dr. Allenby. His number is by the kitchen phone."

The rest of the day was a blur. Dr. Allenby arrived at the same time that an ambulance pulled into the driveway. He had already called the pastor of the Presbyterian church across the street. At the hospital, Dr. Allenby brought the terrible news, "Jim's gone, Carolyn. It was a massive heart attack. I'll take you home."

As they entered the empty house, Carolyn, in a daze of shock, said, "I need to call the children, and Augusta."

She went to the kitchen phone and put a call through to Kate, in North Carolina. She spoke the difficult words, "Kate, your father died this morning."

"Mama, No!" Kate's heart-rending scream brought her husband, Jerry, who took the phone and after a few seconds said, "Of course we'll come. We'll get there as soon as we can."

A little later, as 18-month-old Sarah napped and Jerry talked with his boss, Kate tried to get her thoughts together and pack their bags for the long, sorrowful trip. A poignant memory stabbed her heart as she folded clothes and placed them in the open suitcase. She and her father were in Montreat for a conference, the summer before her wedding. They piled bags into the car and started down the winding mountain road. Her father had put his hand on her knee and said, happily, "Gal, let's go home."

Now, Kate whispered through her tears, "Oh, Father, you're finally Home."

Getting word to James was more difficult, and Carolyn relied on her pastor, who had arrived when she returned from the hospital. James, his wife Joan and two young children were living in Germany, where he was stationed with the United States Army. The pastor finally got through to the International Red Cross, who promised that James would be notified of his father's death, and brought home as soon as possible.

Sometime during that terrible afternoon, Carolyn looked up to see that her dear friend Marilyn, a member of the church, had come in.

"Carolyn, dear, you need to take this medication the doctor left, and eat a little of this soup I brought you." She helped Carolyn to her bed, and talked to her until she fell into a fitful sleep.

The doorbell rang often as did the telephone. Marilyn welcomed friends and took messages. Before dinner time, the house was full of people, and food overflowed the dining room table.

Around six, Sophie's soft voice woke Carolyn. "Miss Woolridge, Miss Little's here. I'm leaving now. I'll be back tomorrow."

Through the fog of blinding grief, Carolyn murmured, "Augusta can take care of things." A few moments later she fell into her sister's arms and they wept. Augusta helped her get dressed, so she could speak to the people gathered in the living room.

Around midnight, Kate and her family arrived, after a ten-hour trip. Augusta had made up the guest room for them, setting up the antique crib for Sarah. In the days that followed, the curly-headed toddler, oblivious to the sadness, gloried in extra attention, and served as a much-needed distraction for her grandmother.

All the next day, people came by—pastors from the Presbytery, friends in her church, and neighbors. More than once, Carolyn heard herself say, "I'll tell Jim you're here," only to be overcome with the horrible realization that Jim was not in his study waiting for the visitor.

One thoughtful friend brought a rag doll she made for Sarah. After visiting with Kate and Sarah, she told Carolyn, "I want to come and stay here with her during the service," and she did.

John, Carolyn's pastor, helped the family plan a funeral service, delayed for nearly a week, until James arrived.

Six days after Jim's death, Carolyn, surrounded by her family, celebrated the faithful life of husband, father and pastor.

"These are they which have come out of great tribulation and have washed their robes and made them white in the blood of the Lamb," the pastor read, from Revelation 7:14 (NIV). A sense of glory filled the small stone church, as pastors and Presbytery and Synod leaders spoke of the work and legacy of a man of God who had finished his work and been called Home. Standing to recite the Apostles' Creed, they affirmed their belief in "the forgiveness of sins, the resurrection of the body, and the life everlasting."

Carolyn spoke to every person who came, amazed even through her grief, at the impact Jim had made on hundreds of lives.

The Reverend James Craig Woolridge II was buried in a family plot in Anniston, Alabama. He died on March 11,1961, at fifty-nine years of age. March 18, 1961 marked the thirty-first wedding anniversary of Carolyn and Jim Woolridge.

A week after the burial, a lonely visitor appeared at the front door. Holding his hat in his hand, he said quietly, "Mrs. Woolridge, you don't know me. I'm the pastor of the A. M. E.

Zion Church up on the hill."

Carolyn and Kate welcomed the man into the living room. He sat uncomfortably on the edge of a chair, still holding his hat.

"I had to come," he said quietly, "when I saw in the paper that Doctor Woolridge had died." His voice quivered, and he waited a moment before speaking again. "I couldn't believe it. It couldn't be 'our' Mr. Woolridge!"

Kate offered the gentleman a cup of coffee. He shook his head. "I . . . can't stay long. Some thought I shouldn't come. Things being what they are, it's dangerous for you." Kate understood, recalling last night's news of Civil Rights protests beginning to sweep across Alabama and the South.

Carolyn touched the wrinkled hand. "We're not worried about any danger. We appreciate your coming to pay your respects."

He looked at her. "You don't understand. You see, Mr. Woolridge came to our church every week."

Carolyn blinked. "I never knew that."

"No, Ma'am, he wouldn't have talked about it." He took a deep breath. "Our little school, at the church, doesn't have any money, but we have children who want to learn. Somehow Mr. Woolridge found out about us and he just showed up one day, about two years ago, and asked if he could teach history to our young people. He came every week and our children couldn't get enough of listening to him."

The lined face broke into a smile. "He could make them laugh, but they learned all about history. European, American, and the history of Christianity. When we asked him why he came to our school, he just said, 'I love history'."

He hung his head, then brushed a tear from his cheek. "Now he's gone to glory." He looked up. "But we'll probably never know how many of our young folks had their lives changed by this good man who cared enough to risk his life to come and teach them. They saw what a true man of God looked and acted like, and they want to be like him. Most of them got no daddy, but they had Mr. Woolridge. He was always taking time to talk to them, listen to their troubles." The soft gray head went into his hands. "Now we done lost him."

At that moment, Kate was thinking of Pastor Shelby and the congregation of Smith Memorial. She couldn't stop a smile, as she thought of her father and the other pastor laughing on the front porch, that Sunday morning.

Carolyn was remembering Jim, in his clerical robe, taking a tiny baby into his arms, and claiming the promises of Covenant baptism for her. That same day he ordained her father as a minister of the Gospel and welcomed him into the fellowship of pastors in North Alabama Presbytery.

A week later, Kate and her family went back to North Carolina, leaving James—on a month-long bereavement leave—to shepherd his mother through the details of probate and moving out of the Presbytery's Manse, into the Anniston home of her girlhood which she would share with Augusta for the next twenty years.

Abraham of old answered God's call to leave his home in Ur of the Chaldeans, claiming God's Covenant promise of the establishment of a great nation (Genesis 12:1-3). Jonathan Woolridge left his home in Nyack, New York, and followed the call of God to Hampden-Sydney College and Union Theological Seminary, to become a traveling pastor and church planter in the coal fields of Southwestern Virginia. He later pastored four congregations in North Carolina, inspiring his only son to obey the call to Gospel ministry.

In answer to his mother's prayer before his birth, God called Jim Woolridge to be a pastor to four congregations, and two Presbyteries in the Southern Presbyterian Church, during thirty years of ministry.

In the American South, from 1930 until 1961, though it was economically difficult, and often dangerous, Jim Woolridge preached and lived out the Gospel of Jesus Christ because he served his Master with a passion for obedience to God's Word, and with a Pastor's heart.

James Wool, student at Union Theological Seminary, Richmond, Virginia

Caroline O'Bryant, student at General Assembly's Training School, Richmond, Virginia

Caroline O'Bryant in wedding dress,
Stuart's Draft, Virginia, March 18, 1931

Caroline's Mother, Annie O'Bryant ready to give the bride away. March 18, 1931

Telegram announcing the birth of
Katharine Augusta Wool,
Stuart's Draft, Virginia, February 15, 1933

Katharine at one year, on Grandmother O'Bryant's lap,
Uniontown Presbyterian Church in background

*Presbyterian Church,
Marlinton, West Virginia*

*Jim and Caroline Wool,
Marlinton, West Virginia*

*James Craig Wool III, born October 23, 1937
(2 years old here)*

*Katharine Augusta Wool in backyard of Marlinton
manse ("switch tree" in background) circa 1941*

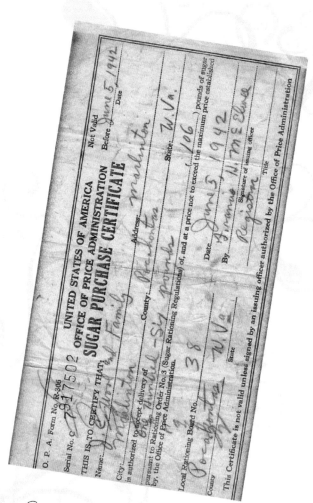

Sugar rationing certificate during World War II for a family of 4 for the entire year.

Katharine Augusta Wool
Cary High School, Cary, North Carolina

James Craig Wool III, drum major uniform
Cary High School, Cary, North Carolina

*Caroline O'Bryant Wool
(portrait probably taken in Guntersville, Alabama)*

*Dr. James Craig Wool III, Executive Secretary,
North Alabama Presbytery, 1960*

Tar Baby, Cocker Spaniel,
beloved family pet.

"We must go through many hardships
to enter the kingdom of God."
Acts 14:22b NIV

A note from the Author

The characters in this narrative are real people. Though the fictional nature of the writing created the need for name changes, dates and historical events in the lives of people are accurate, based on research into family, church, presbytery, county, cemetery and city records. This is Jim Wool's story, beginning with the ministry of his father.

Born in 1858, John Ellis Wool answered the call to Gospel ministry in the late 1880's, and traveled by train to small towns in the coal fields of Southwest Virginia, establishing as many as six churches in the area. He married Katharine Rachella Kelly of Tazewell, Virginia in June of 1900, and they moved into the manse beside Oxford, North Carolina's Presbyterian Church. A year later, Katharine died after giving birth to a son, James Craig Wool II. John later married Annie Bullock Webb, of Stem, North Carolina, and five years later the family moved to Wilson, North Carolina, where John was pastor of the First Presbyterian Church. Later, he ministered in churches in Mecklenburg Presbytery, serving on church courts and commissions. He died on March 18, 1922, in Jackson, Mississippi.

A few weeks after his father's death, James graduated from Davidson College, and went on to Union Theological Seminary, in Richmond, Virginia. There he met Caroline O'Bryant, of Anniston, Alabama, who was a student at the Presbyterian General Assembly's

Training School across the street. They were married in 1931, in Finley Memorial Presbyterian Church, near Staunton, Virginia, where Jim was the pastor. Their first child, Katharine Augusta Wool, was born in 1933, and a few months later, the family moved to the Presbyterian manse in Uniontown, Alabama. Their second child, James Craig Wool III, was born there. Later the family moved to Marlinton, West Virginia, where Jim served the Presbyterian church, as well as two small mountain congregations, for eight years, during the time of World War II. From there the family moved to North Carolina, where Jim was Executive Secretary of Granville Presbytery. Later came a pastorate in Bishopville, South Carolina, and another Presbytery position in North Alabama, where he died in 1961.

Fictional stories of courtships, weddings, baptisms, church problems, funerals, family traditions and hardships interlaced the family narrative, making the story come alive for the reader. They showcase the faithful dedication of a man of God, who faced discouragement, trials—even death threats—to serve His Savior and Lord, Jesus Christ, in the tumult that was the American South, in the mid-twentieth century.

The tale of interaction and dialogue across three generations is filled with excitement, laughter and strong family ties. As Anna Kate unearths a treasured family heirloom and learns its hundred-year-old story, she discovers the meaning of faith and family.

ASIN: 1493599771

Songs of the Seasons
Songs of Family
Songs of Devotion
Nonsense Songs

ASIN: 1456347055

We need the first hand stories of people who have traveled a road. I'm sure this lovely book will be a guide and comfort to many who find themselves alone - and not ready.

Margaret Jensen, author

ASIN: 1456520792